LEARNING
THE GAME

LEARNING THE GAME

Kevin Waltman

SCHOLASTIC PRESS

NEW YORK

Thank you to Vince Masterson for wading through the earliest and roughest beginnings of this effort. Thank you to the baristas at Bad Ass Coffee in Tuscaloosa, who kept me caffeinated enough to crank out the pages. And thank you, of course, to David Levithan, whose efforts and encouragement made this possible.

Library of Congress Cataloging-in-Publication Data Available

ISBN 0-439-73109-7

12 11 10 9 8 7 6 5 4 3 2 1   5 6 7 8 9/0

Printed in the U.S.A.   37
First edition, July 2005

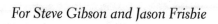

For Steve Gibson and Jason Frisbie

Chapter 1

The one thing I can do is shoot. People know this. But Luke leaves me open on the wing — mistake. Jackson kicks to me and, as natural as a heart pumping blood, I fire, follow through, bury another J, the ball ripping through with a crisp sound. Yes, one thing I can do is shoot the ball.

"Nice stroke, Nate," Jackson tells me, and we bump fists.

Come November, I'll be in a battle for playing time — Coach Harper wants me to improve my ball handling, defense, conditioning — all those things that don't come as easy as my jump shot. Personally, I think we need a shooter like me on the floor, but I know how to play Coach's game, too, so I never say a word. For now, though, it's open season: We have enough to run full-court, no subs, as long as the sun lights the court behind Sigma Chi, one of the fraternities at the local college. Like the other frats, it's vacant over summer, the open court an invitation to us now, though during the school year none of us would ever approach the place; to the college kids we're just high school townies, at best an inconvenience to their good time. When they leave, though, the town is ours — as it should be — and every day we're at the court. The frat itself is huge, one of five on the block, but all the other houses and apartments here are run down, some with broken windows, some with litter-strewn lawns, properties my parents say are brought down by being so close to a frat. Last I knew, my brother had moved into one of these places.

My folks don't make me work — really, they don't *make* me do anything anymore, since they'd actually have to turn off the TV and get out of their chairs to do that — so I get here earlier than the others, giving me more time to fine-tune the J. I start in close, making sure my form is straight, refamiliarizing my hands with the feel of the leather, the dimples on the ball worn almost smooth as my fingers. I let my body find that fluid rhythm of knees–elbows–wrist, one flowing gently to the next until the shot is almost an organic extension of my body. Then I move in small arcs away from the hoop: ten feet, then twelve, then fifteen, then stepping out to twenty. Once I get warmed up it's just bucket, bucket, bucket — not even touching the rim. Smooth. What I work on these days is pull-up jumpers and fadeaways, shots where I have to hurry a bit, working on holding form even when I'm off-balance, leaning back until I can feel my muscles flex all the way up to my shoulders. Bucket, bucket. I'm gaining strength, too, which helps my chances. Today I put in a full hour before the other guys show.

Luke has the ball now, but he can't get by me — a good thing, since I'll be competing with him this season. If I can make myself a little less one-dimensional, I have a shot to start. He dumps the rock down to Saveen in the post, who rises effortlessly and floats in a turnaround. A senior, Saveen will be a starter for the third year in a row, no sweat, probably one of the best players in the county this year. He grabs the ball as it drops through the net and thumps it on the blacktop once, then stares at his teammates. "Next point wins," he says. "Let's D up."

Along with Saveen, Jackson and Trey are sure-fire starters — Jackson at point guard and Trey at forward. The last two spots are a fight for three players: me, Luke, and a senior named Brian Branson, a guy who hardly ever plays with us during summer. Branson's a scrapper and a borderline dirty player on the floor, but Coach Harper loves him, always giving him more minutes than he probably deserves. The rest of the players here will be scrambling to steal playing time from one another or to contribute in whatever way they can. Some of the guys here might not even make the team, their minutes snatched away by promising freshmen, though we never let guys that young run with us during the summer.

Jackson drives and tries a little runner, but Saveen blocks it, pounding it like a bass drum. I race Luke to recover the loose ball, both of us trying to gain control without going out-of-bounds. We collide, and Luke loses his balance, careens into an old bike that's been rusting all summer in the fraternity weeds. I turn and set my feet, alone in the corner. The afternoon sun is hanging at a nasty angle, casting a glare so I can't really see the rim — I just have to shoot from memory and a feel for my spot on the court.

I've fired this shot thousands of times, practicing by myself, playing pickup with my brother as a kid, playing horse with my girlfriend, Lorrie, even last year as a starter for the junior varsity — so much repetition that time slows when I'm open like this, and an image of future glory flickers through my mind, Jackson kicking it to me under the lights, both of us in the blue-trimmed varsity uniforms, a game on the line. And it comes down to me. I let it go, then lose sight of its arc in the sun. I *hear* it go in, that perfect ripple of a ball through the net, the purest sound this world offers. I can feel the burn of small blisters on my feet, the tang of my own sweat in my mouth, the dull ache of my knees after a day on the court. All of it feeling just right.

"Ball game," Jackson says. "Way to be, Nate."

My imagination is still playing out its own scene, too, like the real shot I just hit isn't enough. I imagine Jackson racing to hug me in victory, our picture captured for the paper's front page, the classic sight of the backcourt combining to send the crowd into a court-rushing frenzy.

Behind me, though, rising from the weeds, Luke disputes the play. "Wave that off," he says. "That was a foul."

"Where?" I say.

"On the loose ball. You elbowed me out."

There's a chorus of protests from my teammates — calls of *bullshit* and *no blood, no foul.*

Saveen, Luke's own teammate, settles it. "That's a clean play and you know it. Just because you can't guard the guy is no reason to make excuses." Nobody argues with Saveen, who's six-five and still growing. "Good shot, Nate. Mighty." He slaps

4

me five, and I have to hide my excitement — approval from Saveen is rare. "Boy can shoot," he says to whoever cares to hear. Luke sulks to the far end of the court and slams back the last of his water. He squeezes the bottle, the plastic crinkling, and he hurls it toward the frat. It slips cleanly through a window on the second floor. "Figures I make *that* shot," he says. He rips off his shirt, mops the sweat from his face and neck.

It feels good to get under his skin a little. Lord knows I've put in the hours.

We run a few more games, but they're not as competitive. We dissolve into trying more difficult shots and passes as the games go on, looking for one last spectacular play before we call it a day. The matchups are entirely flexible, so after squaring off against Luke in one game I'm helping him contain Jackson in the next. We try to separate Saveen and Trey, and by the end of each day we disintegrate into letting them showboat, trying to set them up for dunks, even though Trey usually sends his skimming over the bucket or getting stuffed by the rim.

I don't hit as many shots in the last few games, my legs tiring, but for the last bucket of the day I knife into the lane with a crossover even Jackson would be proud of and hit a little runner.

"Branson better get himself out here, or he'll be watching those moves from the bench," I say. I don't usually talk trash, but I know I've put together a nice string of games. I give a glance at Luke, who just returns my stare, a look on his face like more than the sun is burning it.

"You're still just a shooter, Nate," he says. "Don't get carried away because you had one good day on the blacktop."

"You had a hard enough time trying to stick me."

Luke starts to say something but hesitates, kicks at the edge of the court, where I can see bits of glass in the shale. He looks at me again, his eyes sharp and cold. "You got about as much chance of starting next year as your brother does of getting elected sheriff."

The other guys, chugging water or still practicing a few extra shots at the other end, stop. There are a few murmurs before somebody says, "No need for that, Luke." Only I don't see who says it because I've already started for my car. Shots at my brother, Marvin, are not things I take lightly.

The car has a heat that feels like a violent, breathing organism from baking all afternoon. The sweat that had started to dry reawakens in long streams down my body and face, and for a moment I think I might actually suffocate in my parents' ride, my body slumped against the dash, defeated by an Indiana summer. Everything I touch in the car burns: the wheel, the metal at the ignition, even the plastic levers for the AC. I get it started and throw it into reverse — another burn on the gearshift — wanting to escape as fast as possible, get away from what Luke said. I should have given him a quick pop in the mouth, but I have to play by the rules, pretend like I'm above that, or else word will get back to Coach Harper — never mind that Luke could probably handle me if it came to a fight.

There's a knock on the window, a body moving with the car as I back out. Luke. There's an impulse to just peel away, spray him with gravel, but I stop, compelled by the regret on his face. I slam the car into park and roll down the window.

"Yeah?"

"I'm sorry, Nate. I shouldn't have said that."

"That it?" I start to put the window back up.

Luke puts his hand in on top of the window, and I'm tempted just to keep rolling it up, pinching his fingers right down to the bone. But I don't, again backing down. "I was just pissed because I didn't play well. No excuse, I know."

I don't say anything, not wanting to give him satisfaction.

"All that stuff on the court? You know come this fall I'm your teammate, no matter who's getting playing time." He sticks his hand inside the window, extending it like a paper to sign.

I give him a quick five, deciding to let him off the hook. "Don't sweat it, man. I'll catch you tomorrow."

He taps the roof of my car as a good-bye, and I wheel away, my hands still tender on the steering wheel's heat. I ease down the alley, weaving around potholes, wondering if one of the windows facing the alley is Marvin's room, though everything about him — where he lives, where he works, how unstable he is — is as much a rumor to me as it is to anyone else.

Five years ago, when he was fifteen, Marvin killed his best friend. I hate to put it that way: *killed.* It makes it sound like he meant to do it. We were at the Hartwells' house during the summer. Marvin was friends with their older son, Jeff, and I would play basketball with Ray, the younger one, even though I was already worlds better than he was. When the gun went off, Ray and I were outside and I knew instantly what it was, even though I'd never heard a gunshot that wasn't in a movie or on television. Ray didn't know, though; I could tell. He just stood there with the ball in his hand, staring at the upstairs window where the sound had come from, his tongue dabbing his lips like he was trying to identify a taste rather than a sound.

Ray looked at me. "Just someone slamming a door," I said. I didn't want to admit it was a gunshot, like delaying the truth long enough might reverse it completely. The shot echoed through the neighborhood, though, and Mr. Gaston waddled over, a dirty towel slung over his shoulder. He was determined to drag the truth out of the house, and what he dragged out was one dead teenager, Mr. Hartwell's pistol minus one bullet, and my brother. Marvin's body looked changed, loose and vacant. Like he was dead, too.

It is something I don't like to dwell on, but it always dances around the edges of my thoughts, like flashes of light in peripheral vision. It takes the whole drive home before I can push those images away far enough, like cramming a trunk of old clothes in the deepest corner of an attic.

Nobody is in the house when I get home, and I dial Lorrie's number, hoping to score alone time with her. No answer, though, and I leave no message — I don't trust my voice on her parents' answering machine, like it will reveal some lust her parents haven't considered yet. I flip on the big-screen, looking for something to keep my mind from Marvin, but the television is a depressing sight on a late-summer afternoon: boy-band videos, news updates, black-and-white movies, baseball. No thanks.

I try to think hoops again, replaying my daydream of hitting a game winner. I try sorting every player into a depth chart, rationalizing ways I can make the starting five. But what keeps intruding on my thoughts is the image of Marvin walking out of that house, the sound of the single shot ripping through the air, through my memory — there was the way I remember things before that shot and the way I remember things after.

It's not long before Jackson saves me by knocking at the door, peeking through the little triangle my mom's lace curtains create.

"You cool?" he asks, walking in.

"Sure," I say.

We head straight to the kitchen and wordlessly pillage my mom's groceries: sodas, microwave burritos, ice-cream bars, barbecue chips, pasta salad, oranges, crackers, pepper cheese. We lay it all out on paper towels on the counter and start into the food indiscriminately, not giving any mind to the strange mix of tastes we've collected. Jackson tears open a sleeve of cookies, and they roll like loose change onto the counter.

"I just wanted to make sure you were okay with today. That wasn't right, what Luke said."

"Not a thing," I say. "I just keep thinking it's over, that it's been long enough that people have forgotten about it. Then someone brings it back up."

"You pissed at Luke?"

9

I grab one of the cookies, pop it whole into my mouth. Then I say through a cloud of crumbs, "How can I get pissed at someone I used up on the court today?"

Jackson bumps fists with me, laughs.

"I'm telling you, man," he says, "you step up like that and we could have a run at county, maybe more. Mighty."

"It'll take more than that," I say.

"Well, I figure I've got point, and you know Saveen is the best big man around. We get you going and even Coach Harper can't mess us up. Guy couldn't coach his way out of a wet paper bag, but we'll be good."

Stuffed, we leave the rest of the food on the counter and head to the pool. I dangle my feet in and Jackson leans over the edge to pull a raft up, then floats toward the center. When he gets out there he pulls his shirt off and throws it in a perfect arc toward the basket at the side of the pool. "Bucket," he says when it drops in.

"You really think I can play in front of Branson?" I say.

Jackson squints at me. "Branson. That guy. Pisses me off the way the coaches think he's so good. He's the only trouble-maker we have, but the coaches love him because they think he's *hard-nosed.*"

"You have to admit," I say, "Branson is a tough kid." I like the fact that Jackson dislikes Branson, and I know it doesn't hurt my chances that our point guard favors me.

"Shit," Jackson says, spitting the word at me. "If Branson's ass was black they'd kick him off the team instead of talking about how gritty and tough he is."

Jackson cocks his head at me, daring me to challenge his statement, but I'm not going to argue with him on that point.

Later we move inside to throw in a DVD. While we're choosing one, Jackson pries about Lorrie, asking if things are still smooth with her. I tell him to mind his own business, but then I tell him that I've got everyone fooled, that in her world I am honor roll and jump shot and milk and honey all wrapped up into one.

"Well, that's what you are, schoolboy. Learn to know yourself," Jackson says. He is nothing if not direct, and I like him for it. We've really been friends for only a year, but basketball has brought us closer, especially this summer, and I'd love nothing more than to have a couple good years on the court with Jackson and me running the show.

I pull down a stack of DVDs and spread them on the table in front of Jackson, who's reclining in my father's leather chair.

"What do you want?" I ask. I know it will come down to *Hoosiers* or *Hoop Dreams* or possibly an action movie. That basically constitutes the entirety of our movie taste, even though my parents have more than two hundred DVDs to choose from.

"I don't know. Don't say *Lethal Weapon* again, but I can't choose. You have too many, Nate. Too many DVDs. Your parents are loaded, you know that? Loaded."

11

He's right again. My parents have been rich for as long as I can remember — rich and sad and miserable for the last five years.

Jackson throws his hands behind his head and yawns. "I think I might just move in here. Become a new member of the Gilman family. Think your parents will go for that?"

We laugh at the notion, but he is so at ease in our space now that it seems almost plausible, the lines between us starting to blur. It makes me want this summer to last forever, but the calendar insists there is just one week left until they rein us back in, jar us from the days we schedule for ourselves. They will seat us in orderly rows, from which we are supposed to learn. We will be herded back to school, where they think I am honor roll and jump shot, milk and honey — or at least the Gilman boy who isn't Marvin.

Chapter 2

My mom's purse is on the table, so I help myself to a twenty before I go. I walk through the living room where they're watching TV and tell them not to wait up. My father raises his head and offers me a feeble smile. My mom mutters that I should be careful but have a good time. Since they've become this way I just take what I need — the car, extra cash — and break what I don't — curfew. I can't help but wonder what it would take to wake them from their numb little worlds, but I don't ask questions.

My dad is a big shot at a large construction firm, one of only a handful of men who work there and wear a suit every day, and my mom comes from money, her grandfather a forgotten but well-financed name in publishing. Together it's quite an income, I suppose, though neither of them really *does* anything anymore. My dad has an office to go to, and my mom has her weekend trips so she can "get away and relax." To be fair, they were not always this way, but the memory of them as people who talked or yelled or laughed or cared about anything is getting dim.

Marvin, even though he hasn't lived here in years, is always a presence. We don't speak his name, but it is the unspoken word haunting every conversation. And it wasn't just Marvin's accident that defeated my parents — the majority of it, yes, but it was made worse by all the small disgraces that followed it, the school suspensions and arrests and endless arguments. Eventually, they gave up. They let Marvin slip out of our lives, even though he is never really gone.

I hop in the car — my dad had it washed, so it's looking smooth and sleek for the weekend — and head to Lorrie's. It's now the last Saturday night before school starts, so everyone will be out. Even though I'm still getting used to having my license, every time I drive I worry a little less about following the book to the letter. I figure if the cops pull me over they'll just give me a warning. They know the Gilman name in town. My dad's company gets every big project, namely because he was college roommates with the mayor, so I'm not treated like just another kid in Cheneysburg.

That goes for Lorrie's parents, too. When I get to her place her dad gives me a bone-crunching handshake, then squeezes my shoulder to the point of pain. I know it's just his game, and I pretend to enjoy it, like he's one of the guys.

"How's that jumper, Nate? Lorrie says you've been playing every day."

"Straight and true, Mr. McIntyre."

He goes upstairs to get Lorrie, and Mrs. McIntyre calls me into the kitchen, inquiring about the approaching school year. I answer like I'm downright excited to head back to

Cheneysburg High, like trig and bio and world history are the three greatest things a kid my age could hope for. Mrs. McIntyre trusts me, but in an entirely different way from her husband. She's wary of everything basketball, especially since Lorrie plays on the girls' team at school. While Mr. McIntyre cheers proudly, I think Mrs. McIntyre wishes her daughter were the one cheering, leaving the athletics to the men.

"What are you and Lorrie doing tonight?" she asks.

"We're going to Trey's to watch a movie." A lie. We're going to cruise through town and then go somewhere to fool around like always. But that's the beautiful thing about Mrs. McIntyre: She doesn't like her daughter playing basketball because she believes in certain truths about the way things should be, and those truths also say that a kid on the honor roll is incapable of lying. That kind of truth doesn't work in my world, though. I'm long past believing in any of that — except on the court, where the rules make sense. But I'd never let on to Mrs. McIntyre or any other adult. As far as she knows, what she believes in me is unshakable gospel, and I am the perfect boy to trust with her only child.

Waiting in her kitchen makes me nervous, like one wrong syllable will reveal everything. So when she asks me about my parents, about my mother's health and my father's business, I try to keep the answers simple: They're fine; she still gets fatigue, but she's better; business is great.

Then Lorrie is ready, and we're out the door. Almost. Mrs. McIntyre doesn't like that Lorrie is wearing a "ratty old T-shirt"

15

to go on a date. As far as I'm concerned, what Lorrie wears makes no difference. We've been dating for two years now, so there's no reason for Lorrie to put on a show for me — that's what I like about her; she is who she is. It lets me feel natural with her, too.

Besides, she still looks fine in a T-shirt. More than fine. She's tan from a summer of basketball and swimming, her hair pulled back to show off her face: high cheekbones, brown eyes with a smolder beneath them. Everything about her always looks just right, athletic and orderly, no matter what she wears.

It's her mom's orders, though, and Lorrie goes back upstairs to put on something "proper," which after a few minutes turns out to be a pullover blouse that shows off her midriff — more revealing by far, but somehow Mrs. McIntyre isn't worried about that, as the blouse meets with approval.

As soon as we're in the car, though, Lorrie whips out the T-shirt, which she had balled up under the blouse and pinned against her side by her elbow. She throws it on over her top and then, tucking her arms inside her sleeves, slithers out of the blouse and pulls it off, the T-shirt concealing her the whole time. It's like a striptease happening right in front of me, but not revealing any of the essentials.

"I can't stand this thing," she says. She wads the blouse up and sets it on the dash. "It itches like crazy. Just remind me to put it back on, though, before I go home."

I'm still thinking about her nimble display of taking it off. The streetlights shine in her window and make a light sheen on her arms and cheeks. She has her hair pulled up tonight, and her neck looks fragile and tempting. "Sure, I'll remind you. How could I forget? You think you could try that routine again, though, a little slower this time? Maybe without the T-shirt over top?"

She leans her seat back and puts both feet on the dash, stretching her legs out and rubbing them gently together at the knees. "Nothing you haven't seen before. Just keep driving — let's meet up with the crew down at Kwik Mart."

I cruise down the main strip, weaving through the traffic — it's all kids out driving the same route, even kids from the other county schools. The cars move constantly up and down the drag, the parking lots of Ridge's Hardware and Alger's Market serving as turnarounds, the anchors at the north and south ends of the strip. Along the way we see small groups gather in parking lots, a few cars in front of the grocery store, some recognizable faces gathered at a fast-food joint, and our crew, which is growing bigger and more popular all the time, at Kwik Mart. Luke, Saveen, Trey — they're all there with girlfriends in tow. There are some younger kids, too, those freshmen- and sophomores-to-be who show enough social promise, usually through the grades and good recommendations of older siblings, to be invited out. You can always tell they're nervous, , though, especially around Saveen.

The only one missing is Jackson, which is no surprise. As tight as he is with me, he can disappear for entire weekends, like he has a secret life somewhere else, or a distrust of the

Cheneysburg social scene beyond the basketball court. Whenever I ask he just shrugs it off. I suspect he isolates himself because he's one of the only black guys our age in town, but I've never known quite how to ask about that — it is the one divide remaining between us, one we don't really talk about, but there have been moments I've felt that distance start to disappear as mysteriously and silently as it arose. Tonight he and I were going to get together, but when I called him to say Lorrie wanted to go out, the distance was there again, a thick silence when I told him to come with us, which he finally broke by saying, "No, it's not my thing. Third wheel, you know."

While I wish Jackson was here, there's one person I could do without: Branson. He's unmistakable — a scraggly starter goatee, his hair buzzed short and military, a cigarette dangling from his mouth, the long scar by his right ear looking dark and menacing as it trails down his neck and curls under his shirt. He always seems to have fresh scrapes and cuts on his arms and hands, and tonight one of those hands rests just above his belt buckle on a pint of liquor, the tip sticking out like the butt of a pistol. I kick myself for not noticing his van, a rusted white behemoth that roars like a wounded animal when it runs and has a back stripped of seating except for a couple beanbags so there's more *activity space*, as Branson calls it.

I can smell the alcohol, and I give a quick glance to Lorrie. We're not perfect by any stretch, but neither of us drinks, at least not normally. It's not exactly the best tonic for becoming a better player.

Lorrie notices the same thing, I can tell, but she shrugs it off and gives me a wink. "What other people drink isn't going to kill us," she says.

"Yeah, but Branson might."

She gives me a playful pat on my chest. "You're not scared, are you, Nate? I suppose I'll have to protect you." It's a running joke we have — she's easily as strong as me, but neither of us cares. I suppose my skinny frame should embarrass me most around her, but it's just the opposite: She's the only person I don't feel like I need to prove myself to.

She gives me a soft poke in the small of my back and we move toward the group. We join Saveen and his girlfriend, Candice, who is all hugs for both of us. Candice has always struck me as a bit fake; I just don't trust anyone who's as excited as her all the time. I return the hug, though, as she starts in with Lorrie about how she saw Amy Young at the record store and she was with Robbie Preston, and how it's just an outrage, and by the time that much is out I've moved on to Saveen, bumping fists and nodding.

"What say, Nate?"

"Nada. Just out for the night. Lorrie's folks think we're at Trey's." I point over to Trey, whose arms are slung around his girl-friend, Emma. Behind those two, I see Luke with his hands shoved in his front pockets, looking bored. I catch his eye and we nod at each other, our feud from the other day just ashes now.

Saveen has to look down to speak to me, my eyes just underneath his chin level. "Yeah, I'm about to get out of here.

My parents are out for the night, and I think I'll get Candice alone with me for a while."

I consider asking Saveen if Lorrie and I can join them — a parentless house sounding appealing — but over my shoulder I hear Candice's voice ringing as loud as a fire alarm, and I know the only thing that will happen if we all get together is a whole lot of talking, which is not what Saveen or I have in mind. I look over and see Lorrie laughing with Candice, encouraging her, and I start hoping Saveen makes his move soon. Candice seems to bring out the worst in Lorrie, like her presence creates a smaller, higher-pitched Lorrie that otherwise doesn't exist.

Before Saveen says anything else, though, Branson approaches the two of us, rocking the pint back and forth between his thumb and finger. He takes a quick sip, the bottle coming away to show his lips wet and shiny with the liquor, his tongue rasping a small circle to soak up the alcohol still on his mouth.

"You want?" he asks. He tilts the bottle at me, and I can see the liquid sloshing back and forth inside it. I shake my head and look away, not wanting him to see any fear or hesitation.

He gives the same treatment to Saveen, but when he says, "you want?" it comes out louder, more a public challenge than a question. The whole group, almost a dozen people, looks at the three of us, though they're only really paying attention to Saveen and Branson. Saveen, as far as I know, doesn't drink, and that keeps most of us from doing it, too. There are plenty of opportunities to drink, but it's easy to play by Saveen's rules, to pretend alcohol belongs to another world entirely, one that brushes up against ours but rarely intrudes. Branson, of course, is the wild card. Tough enough to weather fights and scrapes with authority but savvy enough to play it cool when he has to, he runs with every crowd, and he has a knack for introducing new habits — our fist bump is something he picked up from a summer league in Indy, the word *mighty* is a catchall term he brought to us from his stoner friends, and now, perhaps he wants to make alcohol his latest contribution to our scene. I hate the way he infects our actions, our language, but I've never been able to do anything about it.

Saveen looks at the bottle, then back at Branson's face. He raises his hand in Branson's direction but then swats at the air as if he's rejecting a shot in the lane. "Nope. Not my thing," he says.

Saveen winks at me, then walks to Candice, whispers something in her ear, and they are gone arm-in-arm toward Saveen's car.

Branson calls after them, "You hooping tomorrow?"

"Been there every day." Saveen doesn't even look back.

"Mighty," Branson says. He takes another drink. He walks back over and leans on his van, the rust on its sides looking like patches of scorched earth.

After about five minutes without Saveen the crowd starts to get restless, as if they don't know what to do without his bulk as a center of gravity. There's talk of going for pizza, of renting a movie, of driving to another lot where more people might be gathered. I suggest to Lorrie that maybe Saveen's exit should signal ours, too, that it can be a short night out. With Candice gone, Lorrie is back to normal. She says she agrees two hundred percent, sticking her hands in her back pockets so her hips jut out flirtingly.

We drive over back roads, talking about our friends, about wild plans for the future, about our upcoming seasons. "Can you imagine if we both get to start this year?" she says. By *both* she really means me, since she started varsity as a sophomore and scored double figures.

"Do you think people would like us or resent us for it?" I ask.

We're racing out into the country, toward Bethel Bridge, our spot, where the water is choked with debris — old tires, rusty-hinged refrigerator doors, the weather-eaten clothes of who knows how many people who have been there before us. The water runs across it all, sounding like tiny bells in the night, and the moon transforms bits of trash into flecks of silver against the stream's banks. It is a place where the stars and moon give the only available light, the glow from town just a halo in the distance.

"We're not supposed to care what people think," Lorrie says. It seems partly a statement, a warning to me, and partly a theory she's testing. "That's not the point, is it?"

"No," I say. I park by the bridge, the gravel crunching under my slowing tires.

Mostly, we just kiss. Sometimes more than that happens, but it always occurs naturally, neither of us rushing. When we first started dating, I made the mistake of telling some friends that we made out, and when it got back to Lorrie, she almost ended it on the spot. So now, everything is entirely up to her, which means we go a little further all the time — so close this summer that after taking her home I'd lie sleepless in my bed, heart still racing with how close she'd let me. Tonight, though, all I need is Lorrie lying beside me on the hood of the car, the two of us staring up at a night both heavy with heat and laced with a cool ribbon of wind. I can simply turn off for a while, forget everything beyond the two of us. Hours could rush by this way, and I wouldn't even notice.

After all that forgetting, Lorrie still remembers to switch shirts before she goes home, keeping up the illusion for her mother, who may well be waiting on the couch, as she tends to do. I get a few more kisses, and once Lorrie is inside I am alone in the night. I take another spin through town, the strip and the lots emptying now, just small gatherings, drunk boys flexing muscles and threatening fights. Somewhere out there is Branson, while I cruise in silence in my parents' car. I wonder if he is as aware of my presence as I am of his, the two of us each turning the other over in his imagination as we soak up the final weekend of summer.

Chapter 3

Sunday morning we're back at the court — the only churching most of us get — and Branson joins us. As we warm up, he claims to have been out until three thirty, in the generous company of Karen Sumter, a senior-to-be and no stranger to those hours. And though he doesn't mention any particular conquests, Branson wags his thumb toward his van, sitting bone white in the sun, and says, "Karen is friendly, all right."

I shoot at the other end of the court, but he is impossible to ignore. The others laugh at his jokes, feed him passes to help him warm up, and I try to keep track of where all the allegiances stand. Maybe I make too much of it, but I know his cockiness is part of his trick. It fools the coaches into thinking he's a valuable player, and it fools the other players into thinking he's a friend. All except Jackson, of course, who strolls down to my end of the court, dribbling the ball between his legs with each step, giving little jerks and jukes like he might burst into full speed at any moment.

"Don't worry about his ass," Jackson says. "You just play your game, Nate. It's all good, all mighty."

He winces on the last word, recognizing it as a two-syllable tribute to Branson's influence. He grabs me on the shoulder, shakes me back and forth in a rhythm as if he is trying to rattle the sound of that word out of my head. I can feel his fingers pressing on my collarbone, his thumb digging my shoulder. He starts to laugh. "Easy now, killer. We get paired up I'll make you look good."

"I don't need you to make me look good," I say. I turn where I stand and bury a twenty-footer. "Damn, that's pretty," I say. I figure if I talk with confidence, I might play with a little swagger, too, the way my brother would talk trash and strut around the court when we played as kids, before I started getting good enough to challenge him.

As soon as the game starts, though, I can feel that energy start to slip away and get replaced by nerves. It starts with Branson bodying me, backing me down low and then firing a little turnaround. He misses but elevates over me to get his own board, giving a small grunt as his elbow connects with the back of my head. He dumps it in and claps a few times. "Good to be back, boys," he announces. "Good to be back."

On our end Jackson keeps true to his word, driving hard to draw the defense and then kicking it to me for a wide-open twelve-footer. A virtual bunny. I take my time, but the rock feels wrong in my hands, like it's warped and misshapen, and I leave it short. It skirts off the front rim into the hands of Trey, who fires an outlet, and they are off, converting my miss into a quick bucket. In transition, Branson gives me a not-so-subtle elbow and says, "Thought you were a shooter, Nate. That was the best look you'll get on me all day."

In response, I hurry the next one, forcing up a deep jumper with Branson in my face. It barely catches iron, and Saveen gives me a sour look for shooting so quickly. Just like that, my confidence is gone, and at least half of shooting is confidence. When it's rolling, I feel sure of myself, like my fingers extend all the way to the front rim and I'm just dropping the ball in no matter where I am on the floor. But then there are times like this when I get so self-conscious about every little move it's like I'm in a battle without any defense or ammunition, entirely exposed. I trip over my own foot on a jab-step, wrench an extra hitch into my release, lose trust in my own hands. Worse yet, everything in my game flows from my shot, so if *it's* not rolling then it all falls apart: I can't drive by my man if he won't respect my shot; I can't open up passing lanes if people don't have to chase me; and, eventually, I get so worried about the offensive end I lose focus on defense, getting back-cut for easy buckets.

The game ends, mercifully, and though we only lost by two and I got a couple easy hoops to save face, Branson's dominance of me seemed evident. At least to me. As everyone slurps water and swats away mosquitoes, I feel like all eyes are on me, judging. I want the focus on me, I suppose, but I'd rather it be looks of admiration from all the folks in the stands this winter: my parents sitting at a respectful distance from our team's bench; Lorrie near the scorer's table, the blood high in her cheeks from cheering; her parents a few rows up, her father standing and clapping and her mother smiling evenly; the hard-handed laborers from the farms and mills packing the bleachers beneath the north basket; the businessmen who lean on the concourse railings up by the concession stands, still in their suits, their fingers shining with butter from the popcorn; the cheerleaders kicking their legs high, leaving just a slice of fabric between them and the rest of the world; the stoners who, like everyone else, have nothing else to do but go to the basketball games on a Saturday night; the small patch of visiting fans, marking their territory by the color in their sweatshirts; and even the sad lot who stand in the darkness by the corner doors, never taking a seat, shuffling in the shadows, the ones who still come to watch even if the town has chewed them up or refuses to forgive them something from their past, the dropouts, the old yellow-toothed woman you can smell from three blocks away, the small-time dealers who, like talent scouts, eye that group of stoners, and even, sometimes, my brother, Marvin.

But none of that is happening now. Instead, it's Branson looking at me from the other end of the court, the scar on his neck now pinkish, like it's newly sliced.

"That all you got?" He laughs directly at me.

"I'll go again," I say. As much as he got the best of me, he started to slow down near the end, and I know why: He's out of shape. I can see it in the way his chest is still heaving for breath. He can use his mass to his advantage, but after a while it's a burden. "Let's go now," I say, wanting to start the game before he gets rested.

"Hold your damn horses," he says. "You act like you won the fucking game." He starts across the court and walks past me, coming as close as he can without making contact, but I know enough not to flinch. He walks up to the frat house and yanks on a door, which doesn't budge.

"What the hell are you doing?" Saveen calls. "Get down here and play ball."

"I had a friend get me into a party here last year," Branson says. "We got in this way." He jerks the door up, then repeats the motion a few times, yanking harder. Finally, he bends his knees and throws his weight beneath the door, and this time it opens, the darkness beyond it yawning like a cavern. Branson turns to us and smiles. "Mighty," he says. "Come on in, boys. Make yourselves at home." And with that he disappears into the house.

Nobody moves for a second, and I look over to Jackson. He returns my stare, but I can't read him — he just stands there squinting, like he might be in the back of the classroom trying to make out something on the board.

It's Saveen who moves first. He juts his chin out, and his big chest puffs as he starts to march across the court to the house. It's almost like he refuses to bail out on Branson's challenge today after spurning the liquor last night. Of course, Candice isn't here, either; it's just the other guys watching him. Once he moves we all follow.

When we get to the doorway, I see that the bolt has been removed completely, that the only thing holding it closed was a flimsy hook somebody had rigged up on the side of the door, which, courtesy of Branson's force, now lies broken on the carpet. I find Branson at a pool table, racking the balls, as casual as if he lived there.

"You up for a game, Nate?" he says. He leans a cue in my direction. "You were all ready to go a minute ago. You wanna play now?"

I keep my mouth shut, having no idea what the right thing to say could possibly be. I look around and see we have entered the frat's game room: dartboards on the walls, pool and foosball tables, air hockey in the corner, and sloppily built bleacher seating in front of a big-screen TV. The room smells sour and hot, and on the dusty tables I can see cups and bottles that still hold various liquids, cigarette ashes, and small bugs sunk to the bottom.

Branson breaks open a game of pool with a startling *crack*, and half of us jump. But the noise also sets some of the boys in motion. I see Trey wander over to the dartboard, Luke fiddling with the big-screen, which refuses to turn on. Even Jackson starts to mill about, locating some magazines on a corner of one of the bleachers. He picks them up, then seems to think better of it. A few others wander deeper into the house, down the dark internal halls, and I hear them stumble over things as they go. Finally I see light appear from a distant hallway, and a voice calls for us to come check out some discovery.

As a group, we go into the hallway, where there is a composite picture of the fraternity members. They all look alike, more or less, just with different color hair and eyes. Almost without fail, the hair swoops down in a thick part, left to right. The frat boys have an even, uniform smile that matches the white of their shirts, which is set off by red ties and blue blazers. It is hard to believe that we live in the same town as them, though I know that with my father's connections and my own grades I could someday live in a fraternity at a good college, too.

"Pinheads," Branson says, and the rest laugh.

After that, we feel the freedom to explore the house, and there is a rush from nosing through a place where we shouldn't be, a delicious knowledge that we're breaking the rules, especially since we have always resented the presence of the people who live here, the people who invade our movie theaters and restaurants, whose eyes pass over us like we aren't there at all, who for nine months out of a year squeeze us back into a smaller version of our own town. The place is filthy, the walls in each corridor scarred by dents or stains, and there is a faint smell of turned milk. As I wander through the halls, I notice Jackson hanging back at one of the landings, and when we make eye contact he shakes his head at me, then nods toward the exit. I look at the others, though, and their exuberance outweighs Jackson's hesitance. I go on.

It isn't long before somebody tries another unlocked door, this time one of the bedrooms. The shabbiness of the room is too much even for my standards — burns in the carpet, dirty socks stinking in a heap at the center, a tattered curtain barely hanging from a rod to cover the closet, broken glass in the corner, a half loaf of molded bread beside it, flies buzzing on the windowsill. Luke and Trey are the first two in, and all they do is snoop, quickly finding a stack of skin flicks and a hash pipe in the bottom cabinet of the entertainment center. They dismiss the pipe but immediately start putting one of the pornos into the player, checking the patch cords and power when it doesn't turn on.

"If this is what college is all about, it might be okay after all," Trey says, showing a goofy smile, a grin that he thinks suggests he's joking, but always betrays the fact that underneath he's serious.

"Grow up, you two." It's Saveen, towering over the rest of us, his voice coming out in an authoritative bass. The whole crew is crammed into the room now, all ten of us, even Jackson — though he hangs back at the door. Saveen is trying to show that, once again, he's above us, immune to the intrigue of watching a dirty movie.

"Damn straight," somebody says. I turn and see it's Branson, the last person I expected to take the high road. He steps to Saveen and bumps fists with him. With everyone's attention, he goes on: "Why go for the movie when you can have the whole entertainment center?"

Saveen steps back. "What the hell you saying?"

Branson steps toward Saveen, almost like a boxer chasing an opponent in the ring. "I'm saying we liberate some of these pinheads of their mess."

"You mean steal?"

"Steal. Liberate. Whatever. Either way, it's mighty."

The rest of the crew is staring at the two of them, the air in the room close and rank, a funky mixture of the fraternity's neglect and our own sweating bodies.

"Afraid you'll get caught?" Branson says. "Who's gonna see? College doesn't get back for a week, and the other people around here don't care. Or are too strung out to notice." I think, but can't be sure, that Branson gives a nod toward me, and I feel that hot swell again, wanting to defend what I think is a slight against Marvin. But I settle down. If I acknowledge it, then that will make the insult real.

"It's just wrong," Saveen says.

"Wrong?" Branson throws his hands up in the air. He slaps his own forehead in dismay, then puts his hands by his waist in fists. "What's wrong is the fuckers that live here have all this and don't give a damn. That's how it is with these rich pricks. Got everything. Meanwhile, the rest of this town has squat."

Saveen shakes his head, but around the room I can feel a few guys stir. Not many of them — really, none — have parents like mine. Their homes are mostly in the avenues south of the high school, the street gutters full of debris from the cars that rumble past at night, the houses cracking and peeling, the bedrooms inside boiled to a low fury this time of year, slashed to a bitter cold during winter. I know some of their fathers are unemployed, and I know the bruises on Trey's arms increase in frequency and size each time his father is laid off at the chassis plant. As a few of them nod at Branson's plea, I step back and lower my head.

"What the hell am I gonna do with a DVD player anyway?" Saveen says. "Like my mom's not gonna know it's stolen."

Branson smiles now, knowing he's gaining momentum. "No, man. We don't take it home. We sell it. I can get some money for it over in Indy. We get straight cash, and I'll split it right down the line with each of you. Everyone gets a fair share."

Saveen says nothing then, but I see his eyes swing around the room, taking things in. I think I see his hand twitch. Whether that's an impulse to push back Branson, I can't tell, but despite Saveen's size I don't think it would be an easy battle. The scar on Branson's neck stretches all the way down to one of his broad shoulders, jagging and breaking along the way, and I have seen the tattoos he has on his chest and back. I'm sure he has a high pain threshold.

"This room and all the others that are open," Branson says. "We pull in that cash, you could take little Candice out wherever she wants. Bet she'd love you right up for that."

Saveen twitches again. "Fuck it," he says.

With that it starts. Trey and Luke set in on the entertainment center. Branson orders the others to inspect the house to check other rooms, and the group disperses like trails of smoke billowing away from an explosion.

I see Jackson walking out of the house, and I follow him. At his car, he looks at me and says, "No way, Nate. This is some serious bad news. I'm gone."

I stare down at the ground, feeling the angry August sun on my shoulders. As I lean against Jackson's car, I see Branson emerge from the back door of the fraternity. He kicks around beside it until he finds the right-size rock, then wedges it under the door to prop it open. Then he walks across the court to his van and backs it up to the house, the engine growling into the day. Once he gets it to the house, he opens the back doors of the van, then disappears into the cool dark of the fraternity. A few seconds later, I see Luke emerge with a DVD player and load it into Branson's van.

"Shit. Serious bad news, Nate," Jackson says. He throws his car into gear and pulls away. As I watch him leave, I have the impulse to do the same. I know there's nothing for me here. I can't even work up the indignation of being poor like the other guys, and I know I should just follow Jackson and spend the rest of the day at my pool, willing myself to forget all this. I know I should do that. But I don't. There's almost a gravity to the rest of them, my teammates, and again they have a stronger pull collectively than Jackson does alone. As I walk back toward the house, I can feel Jackson growing more distant, and when his car moves out of sight I feel a sever.

I don't do much inside. Mostly, I watch. I see the rest of my teammates haul out TVs, DVD players, small pieces of furniture, digital cameras, stereos, speakers, all varieties of game consoles, microwaves, anything they can carry. They even take some items that could never be sold, as if swept up in the very momentum of theft, hoisting pool cues, answering machines, telephones, glasses and beer steins and Rollerblades, and, when all else is scuttled away, even books. All of it is crammed into the back of Branson's hot and rusting van, weighing it down until the back tires compress, straining under the very weight of the act. For a moment the whole project is in jeopardy when somebody raises doubts about actually getting the money from Branson, since he is the one who will drive off with all the loot. Branson snuffs it out, though, saying we are all linked together, and the only thing that protects us at this point is trusting one another. "I give you my word you'll get paid," he says. "It'll take some time to sell all the stuff, but you'll get paid." He holds his hand up as if testifying.

In the end, I carry a few crates of CDs to the van. I figure it is, literally, the least I can do. I can show I am trustworthy to the others, yet I don't feel like I really get my hands dirty, since they're the ones who collected the discs from the room and boxed them into the crates.

As I take each crate from the cool of the frat to the sauna of Branson's van, there is only a small sliver of daylight I pass through, the few feet between the back door of the house and the back door of the van. But each time I walk through it, I feel for the second time today that all eyes are on me. Only it's not the eyes of my friends and teammates this time but imagined stares lurking around us somewhere, eyes behind drawn shades and cracked windows, in small clusters of trees, or low in the thick and relentless weeds.

Branson watches like a foreman at a work site, his grimy shirt slung over his shoulder like a towel so he can show off his chest, its muscles and scars and serpentine tattoos. "'Atta boy, Nate," he says. "Way to be a team player."

Chapter 4

The TV is flickering inside, like a night-light to give my parents security. They've chosen to wait for pictures of the lunar eclipse — big excitement in Cheneysburg — on the television, rather than come out to the pool for the real thing. "It's getting chilly," my mother said, hugging her arms to her chest. "You can already feel fall coming."

The water's still warm, though, and Lorrie swims laps, cutting razor-straight lines through the water, accelerating with a leg thrust each time she turns at the wall. She swims in the same manner as she does everything else: without deviation from her course. I can't keep up with her, so I rest along the curving side of the pool, elbows propped on the ledge so the tiny teeth of the concrete dig into my skin. She covers almost half the pool underwater, then takes her time rising for air. She's reverting to the contests we used to have, back when she was one of the guests at my summer pool parties — before we started dating — back when Marvin would terrorize us with cannonballs, and my parents, bronzed from hours in the sun, would supervise from their chairs and try to enjoy the songs we'd blast from the stereo, one of them disappearing now and then to fetch snacks for my friends, cocktails for themselves. After everyone was gone, Lorrie and I would challenge each other: Who could turn a flip off the diving board? Swim a lap the fastest? Swim the farthest without coming up for air?

She coasts off the momentum of her push from the wall, not even kicking underwater, cruising slow and peaceful, as if she's the only person for miles around. I wonder what she thinks down there, if she's even aware of me. Or maybe she's completely thinking of me, staying submerged just long enough to make me nervous. My skin tightens in the night breeze as I watch her, and each time she waits until the perfect moment — the moment I actually do start to get anxious for her to come up — to rise, her head breaking through and her mouth opening in a deep, clean gasp before she takes a few strokes to the other end and starts the process over.

Despite Lorrie's graceful and tantalizing routine, despite the pleasure of warm water on my skin and the memories of lazy summers from my past, I'm distracted by other, more recent memories. It was just a few hours ago I helped my friends and teammates burglarize a fraternity. I'm a *criminal*, I think, as if I expect to feel changed, like my very body should be altered by that word.

The phone rings inside, and I see the shadow of my father moving through the light toward it. When he reaches the kitchen, his silhouette picks up the phone, but instead of talking he looks down at the receiver, shrugs his shoulders, and hangs up.

Lorrie surfaces and swims to me. Her hand strokes my shoulder and I give a little flinch. "What's with you tonight?" she asks.

"Nothing." I lean over and give her a kiss, feel the heat from her body. For a moment I can imagine we are the only ones here, that we have been propelled years through time to find that this is our house, the center of a life that belongs entirely to us. No haunting parents. No silly high school games, the breakups and fights and detentions and popularity contests. No Bransons bullying and shaping our world. But as I write our future on the blank page of imagination, question marks insist on punctuating the lines, the uncertainties of income and location and friends. And — always — the presence of Marvin. Somehow, I imagine him a part of any future I have, even if it's just on the edges of my life as he is now. So instead of trying to answer those questions, I lean into Lorrie and concentrate on her.

She pulls back. "There is definitely something wrong with you tonight. You're right next to me, but you feel like you're a million miles away."

For a moment I consider telling her about the theft, dealing with it before it starts to fester inside me. Secrets are not something I do well when it comes to Lorrie. Maybe it's because she's known me so long; she knew me before Marvin's accident, and was always nearby during the sad episodes that followed. A lot of my friends kept their distance from me in the wake of the accident, like Marvin's misfortune might be contagious, all of us treated with such discomfort that, had it not been for the sheer economics of my dad's position, we would have moved. Lorrie, ever steady, never treated me differently. That's a big reason why we grew closer and started dating, the same reason I have trouble hiding anything from her.

"Just thinking about Marvin," I say, which I suppose is not a total lie.

"You don't ever have to be ashamed of that around me," she says, her kindness doubling my guilt. "You can always talk to me about anything." She kisses me on the cheek. "You can be tough to get to sometimes. It's like there's something you're holding back, like, after all this time, you're still afraid to be honest with me."

"I'm honest with you," I say. I think about what she said in the car the other night, how sometimes it feels she can mean two different things at one time. I wonder if that's how I sound to her now.

She backs off then, putting a couple feet of cold air between us. "I don't mean it that way. I don't know. It's something I can never put my finger on with you, like sometimes there's something inside you that you won't show people, something that wants to stir things up." She laughs then, looks up at the sky, and I see the moonlight on her neck. "God, I don't know what I'm saying." She bobs once, comes up smiling again. "Check on how soon the eclipse starts." Then she curves herself into the water, her body moving in a graceful arc — and it's there again for a second, that image of the future, of how incredible she'll be, because there is a sureness about her even now with moonlight glimmering on her skin. I just hope that I can keep up with her as she hastens, as if toward a destination on a map, into the person she'll become.

A scotch bottle sitting open on the counter is all it takes. That smell, sick and sweet in the air, conjures Marvin's image up like a magic spell, as sure as if he were standing in front of me in the kitchen. Right now, all I'm doing is checking on the clock and hearing my father, his blood thin with that scotch, emitting the first sputters of his snore in the living room, my mother silent beside him, watching the end of a movie. But the scotch has me in a memory from five years ago, a night when my parents were having one of their parties and the house was full of noise. Marvin was a month away from his fifteenth birthday, three months away from his accident. Each time we'd pass through the kitchen, Marvin would dare me to take a shot of the scotch, holding it beneath my nose so the fumes irritated my eyes. With him there, I considered it — I was sure that in Marvin's company I was invincible. But he'd always laugh it off, or maybe we'd hear an adult approaching, their steps heavy and obvious. Or Marvin would wink at me and say we'd better start with a little lighter stuff. Then he'd screw the cap back on and replace the bottle.

Later he'd say, "You wanted that scotch, didn't you?"

"Maybe," I'd answer.

"I can always tell. You got some craziness to you." Then he'd clap my shoulder. "That's a good thing, man. You just stick with me. I'll make sure you learn how to use it."

In the living room, I hear the television's low rumble, the shallow breaths of my parents. In the TV's glow I can even make out the beads of water on their glasses and the tiny twitches in my mother's face, like she's not quite ready to surrender consciousness, unsettled in the introduction of a dream.

I get out of there, disturbed by the smell of scotch and the two ghosts in the living room. I take a few long strides across the deck and leap — my legs have spring from constantly playing, and as I levitate above the water I get that hiccup in my stomach the way I do when I take a hill too fast in my car — then plummet deep into the pool, all the way down until my fingers touch bottom. I turn and kick to the surface, a small fire smoldering in my lungs, then burst into the cold air and take a few strokes toward Lorrie, the shock of the water chasing away all those hauntings from my trip inside.

"Hey there!" Lorrie says. "What's gotten into you?"

I keep moving, not wanting to stop, like if I bring my body to rest, all those unwanted thoughts will catch up to me. I give Lorrie a playful dunk into the water. She comes up wiping her face, and then her elbows and fists start to piston at me, her knees digging my thighs in slow motion underwater, her laugh high and simple, bell-like, the way it rang out when we were young. She jumps on my shoulders and tries to force me under, but I lock my legs, so she might as well be trying to force a tree stump farther into the ground. Instead, Lorrie ends up halfway on top of me, still lunging down onto my shoulders, her arms draped across my face and chest, her stomach vibrating like a drum with each laugh, wet against the back of my head and neck. It takes some effort, but I corral her, lock her in place above me, and *shhh* her until she quiets, a small aftershock of laughter still shaking both of us as she balances there, her weight on my shoulders and her head perched just above mine so her chin digs into me. Then I tilt back, looking straight up to where her face blocks the sky so she can give me a brief, upside-down kiss.

"It's almost time," I say, and we break apart and swim to the deep end, our bodies separate entities again. We tread water there, waiting for the eclipse. Lorrie's face is intent, staring so hard it's like she thinks she can coax the event into being, and I know better than to say anything to interrupt her concentration. Instead, I put one arm on the side and pull her to me, our legs brushing against each other in our slow, fluid kicks.

When it starts, Lorrie puts both elbows on the side so she can lean up out of the pool at an angle, like she might rocket moonward to experience the eclipse up close. I float around behind her and watch the yellow of the moon vanish, like a hole in the sky being sealed. But instead of going completely dark as I expected, like a room's single light being snapped off, the moon's hues change, orange bleeding into red at its core, slowly seeping outward like spilled inks of various colors.

Again I hear the phone ring, and the silhouette of my father stumbles toward it so deliberately I can see the ache. The ritual is the same, though: the retrieval off the hook, the confounded bending of his head toward the receiver, the puzzled replacement of it — another wrong number. This time, though, I feel a strange pity for him, my disappointment in his constant surrendering held at bay, maybe because the eclipse makes everything seem more tender.

Looking back to the sky, I can see the outline of the moon, like the watermark from a glass left out too long. I can hear Lorrie's shallow breaths as she continues to watch. In front of me, her head bobs slightly as she moves with the miniature ripples of the pool. I still have my hand on her arm, the pruning skin on my fingers next to her smoothness. She turns and looks at me, her eyes wide and serious. "It's amazing," she says, like it's a secret.

"I know," I tell her. And it is — the moon, the way Marvin's image keeps washing cold against me, Lorrie's rapt attention, the tiny miracles that happen where our skins meet. Everything — this whole uncertain day hidden in its own shadow.

Chapter 5

The first day at school. Everyone looks new again, revived from a summer and wearing the best they have. Every girl looks better, like the three months away have advanced them by years. The working guys — all tan and flexed from outdoor labor — look less ragged, and even the stoners look ready for a new year even though they're still in the official pothead uniform of battered sandals, frayed jeans, and stained and wrinkled concert T-shirts. The school itself seems warmer, less gloomy, like they spent every day of vacation polishing the floors and erasing the residue of the previous year from the walls. There is a clamor of heels clicking and girls squeaking excited *hellos* — even to the people they don't really give a damn about — and hugging their friends like they've returned home from war. The guys bump fists with one another, trying to play cool in contrast. In the middle of all this, I hear Jackson's voice down the hall.

I close my locker — a good locker bay this year, in the main hall along the courtyard, up from the degrading basement where they store the freshmen and sophomores — and seek him out. I find him leaning on the wall next to the office, talking to two kids, one black and one white, neither of whom I recognize.

"What up, Jackson?" I say. I put my fist out to him and Jackson raises his, but I see a slight hesitation, almost a tic that delays his greeting. He gives a nod of recognition, then turns back to the others.

"So, what's the good word, Jackson?" I say. "You ready for this year?"

"Yeah," he says, like that one syllable is a huge weight he's lifting.

"I don't think I know your friends." I know his attitude stems from what happened at Sigma Chi, but I figure Jackson is just testing me a bit, acting out the little game of detachment he seems to like so much, his distant stare becoming too much of a fixture, especially when we're around other people. When we're alone he usually acts normal, but other times the mask goes up, his eyes like secret messages to be decoded.

"I suppose you don't," he says. Then he squints over my shoulder, like there's something at the other end of the hall demanding attention. "Gotta split for class," he says. He clasps hands with the other two and then brushes past me and punches my shoulder, casual enough to be friendly but just hard enough to carry deeper meaning.

With Jackson gone, the other two, who haven't said a word yet, stare at me like I'm behind a piece of glass. They're younger, I think, and the one is starting to look familiar, maybe a kid I've seen working the counter at the taco joint on the strip, but I can't be sure because they're both entirely anonymous, nothing of note on them at all, like they've come straight out off a production line, content to always be faces in the crowd. As they stare, I feel a little of Jackson's anger linger in me, and I want to say something simple and mean — tell them straight off that they're destined for periphery, jobs in dingy cubicles, small houses, wives who don't make anyone jealous.

"You play on the team, right?" one of them says. "Nate Gilman?"

Immediate guilt. They know who I am, but I don't know them. I'm ashamed for everything I just thought about them — I don't even know where it came from, and it scares me, like something my father would say about the people who work for him. "Yeah, I play with Jackson. Yeah."

I make a quick exit then, still burning, but no longer even sure what I'm upset with, or who. The crowd is thinning now, the hugs are completed, and only a few stragglers are hurrying for class, the drudgery of a school year beginning. And so this is it — the sparkling newness of the first day has lasted exactly ten minutes. Welcome back.

My first class is Geometry II. Fitting. I've always made straight As in math without much effort at all, so it gives me time to daydream about hoops. In fact, Coach Harper always preaches that basketball is a game of angles — passing lanes, defensive positioning, precise cuts. He preaches it like it is the word of God, handed down from the great coaching Bible, even though it is not nearly as simple as the geometry I'll be studying this semester. It's not just a game of angles. It's a game of velocity and arcs and collisions. More than that, a game of timing and pulse and emotion, of communication spoken or silently understood, of friends and nerve and adrenaline. And faith. I have learned that to play well with anyone, you must have true faith in him. Which is what Jackson and I were developing — at least until this past weekend.

Forget that, I tell myself. *Focus.* So I look at Mrs. Marsh at the front of the room, sitting there reading straight from the sheet of paper she's passed out to us. She goes verbatim — requirements, grading scale, participation points, test schedule — just like she's done for every class for every year in memory. I remember Marvin complaining about her back when he went to school, and I've had her for two math classes before, like she's my own personal, monotoned guide through the equations of high school. She looks no different this year, either, because she has always looked old, her gray hair pulled back in a severe bun, her dresses always a single, solid color, hanging straight down from shoulder to calf. We always joke she could pass for Amish, easy.

The only interesting thing about her is that she is missing a finger on her right hand, the middle finger, and when she moves the other fingers on her hand, curling or splaying or drumming against the desk, the stub that's left gives little twitches like it's trying to do it, too. I'm fascinated by it, and sometimes it's the only thing I can pay attention to in class. It's amazing anyone has ever learned a single mathematic formula with that stub stealing attention from her lessons. Even Lorrie, who's unshakable from her studies and always polite, admits she can't help but watch it when she thinks Mrs. Marsh can't see her looking.

Gum pops somewhere in the room, and Mrs. Marsh stops her drone.

"That will be the last of that for this entire semester," she says. "Understood?" Then she puts her head back down and resumes reading from the sheet.

From the back of the room I can see the shoulders start to slouch from boredom, feet starting to shuffle restlessly. Candice has positioned herself right in the center of the room, so she can be the hub of activity, and she's trying to get Saveen's attention as he tries to fit his frame into the tiny desk beside her. Candice passes him a note, and even from two rows back I can see the hearts decorating the margins of the page. Saveen reads it and then looks around to see if anyone is noticing, already embarrassed by his girlfriend. I catch his eye and smile, mocking him a bit. Saveen rolls his eyes and then hands the note back to Candice in a huff. He turns back to me, though, and puts his hands through the motion of a jump shot, letting his middle finger twitch an extra time or two, the way Mrs. Marsh's stump would. That's all it takes for me to start thinking hoops again, considering the very mechanics of shooting a ball without that middle finger — almost impossible, since when I'm really rolling it feels like all my body's efforts are funneled to the tips of my middle three fingers, guiding the ball wherever I want.

Saveen gives me a wink, too, a conspiratorial flourish, and while it gives me a moment of uncertainty — *could somebody see it? will people know what we've done?* — there's a part of me that can't help but take pleasure in it. The theft is our personal secret, something nobody else can touch, and all those people, the teachers and counselors, who look at me and see one of the good kids, can't ever really know me or touch me. I can't help but enjoy this new persona I have. I can't help but admire it, as if it were a newly cut jewel and even the dull abrasions of school, the drone of Mrs. Marsh's lecture, can't diminish its luster.

During the school year, before practice starts, we run game at the park. Not the ideal spot, but if we get there right after school, there is always an open hoop. Besides, with the college kids back, there's no more fraternity court for our use. Also, considering how our time at Sigma Chi ended, we won't be going back there any time soon, students on campus or not.

Before I hit the park, though, I make a pit stop at my place to get changed. The house is vacant, but the television is still on, the Weather Channel humming with no more energy than a Mrs. Marsh lecture. I flick it off and then see a note on the kitchen table: *To the city. Money on the counter for dinner. Be back tonight. Love, Mom.* I look closer at the note, and I think the *Love* looks crammed in between two other lines like an afterthought, or a forgery. My mom's absence doesn't bother me, though. Better for her to be out, maybe trying to enjoy herself, than on the couch in front of the television, into wine she probably uncorked before I was done with fifth period.

On the counter she's left two twenties. Where does she think I eat dinner? I remember being a kid and inflating the price of items — ten bucks for the concession stand at the basketball game, twenty for a CD — and then stockpiling the change to enhance my allowance. But now my mother seems to have lost the very concept of pricing. Not that I'm complaining — maybe I can spend some of this on Lorrie, or maybe spot Jackson for something as a kind of penance for letting him down. I pocket the dough before my dad can get home and see how much she dropped on the counter, and I start changing into my hoops gear and lacing up for the game.

I've got the door open, one sneaker already past the threshold, when the phone rings. I think about skipping out on it, but it could be Lorrie touching base or Jackson looking for a ride to the court, so I reverse pivot and grab the cordless in the kitchen.

When I answer, there's a pause on the other end. *Telemarketer*, I think. My thumb readies to turn off the phone, but then the person on the other line speaks.

"Nate?" The voice comes through the receiver with a slight rasp, but it's propelled with some urgency from the speaker. It's a voice I know from games of one-on-one, from waking me in the middle of night to go downstairs to watch movies we shouldn't, from dares to sneak change from guests' pockets when we were on coat duty at parties.

"Marvin?"

"Is anyone else around?"

"No." I walk back to the door, which I'd left open, then close and bolt it. "What are you doing?"

"Good. We need to talk." His voice is starting to settle, sounding almost casual.

"Christ, Marvin. Where are you? What are you doing?" I start walking upstairs. I check my parents' room, which is hot and empty and immense and smells abandoned, the curtains to the main window hanging loose from one of the hooks, sagging drearily.

"Stop sounding so nervous," he says. "I just need to talk to you."

I check on the room where my father sleeps — no signs of life except the remote and empty cocktail glasses scattered in front of the television. I think about checking the entertainment room and the den and the dining room downstairs, but I know I'm just making myself paranoid; a house couldn't be emptier than this one.

The last time I spoke to Marvin was more than a year ago, when I saw him out on the strip. It was one of the last weekends of my freshman year, and I was out with some friends; Marvin was simply trudging out of a grocery store, eggs, cigarettes, and a six-pack of beer weighing down his plastic bag. His face was yellowish, and he almost walked past me without stopping, his eyes showing a slow recognition. It had already been a year since he'd left the house. One final showdown with my parents after he was suspended from school again — this time for smuggling vodka into the cafeteria — led to a muted truce: He jumped from their nest, with money from them serving as a parachute until he landed. It was like a cold, calculated divorce settlement.

At the time, I begged Marvin not to leave. I stood in his doorway, watching him pack — his CDs, his books, all the things he'd let me borrow, portals that offered glimpses into his world — and tried to think up reasons for him to stay. *Me*, I wanted to say, *Stay for me. You're my guide.* I didn't say that, though, and Marvin never stopped packing, never stopped to even give a proper good-bye. For a few months, he'd come back and visit, trying to show our parents that he was making it, but there were always cracks in his independence: cuts and bruises on his hands, a hungry gauntness in his face, his delayed but inevitable requests for more money. Each time he looked worse, and while I thought that was all the more reason for him to move back home, I had learned there was no convincing Marvin — or my parents — of that.

Then, after a couple months, there was nothing. No visits, no phone calls, just sightings of Marvin around town, the rumors of ruinous behavior. Until I saw him on the strip that last time. The first thing that came to mind wasn't to convince Marvin to come home; instead, my first impulse was to wonder if my friends had seen him, if they were whispering behind our backs as we talked to each other.

I think Marvin recognized that, too — recognized that his own brother, the one he'd taught how to shoot jumpers and how to unlock the parental code on the television, was now ashamed of him. We talked for only a few minutes before the bitterness crept into Marvin's eyes. He'd shrugged, said, "See you around," as if he was accusing me of something. The accusation is in his voice now, too.

"What were you doing the other day?" he asks me.

"What do you mean? What day?" I sit down on the fold-out couch my dad sleeps on.

"The day at the fraternity."

"We play basketball there."

"Not just that." Marvin's voice is getting impatient, like when we were playing one-on-one and I'd keep dribbling, trying different moves until one would finally work. *Jesus*, he'd say, *make up your mind already.* Then I'd zip past him, float in a running bank shot.

"What do you mean?" I ask. I'm almost offended by his tone. More than a year since I've heard his voice and he doesn't even bother with courtesy. I understand we didn't exactly leave things on the best terms, but I wasn't the one who decided to move out. If he can accuse me of being ashamed of him, I could just as easily accuse him of acting shamefully.

I reach into the bottom drawer of the nightstand by the fold-out. I find it — an old picture of Marvin and my father at a Cardinals game years ago. My mother, pregnant with me, took it. Marvin is wearing a Cardinals hat that is about three sizes too big, hanging down over his ears and obscuring his eyes, and my father is tan, looking good as he leans down to kiss the top of

Marvin's head through the hat. That type of comfort looks so foreign that it could be an entirely different family, the stock photo that came in the frame. This is not the relationship between my parents and Marvin that I remember.

After the accident, they made attempts: They got him counseling, tried to keep him involved with school, tried being disciplinarians when all else failed. But it was like he was only there a fraction of the time, his mind always drifting elsewhere, silent at the dinner table, except when he released an outburst at my parents. And then he *really* wasn't there. Though I protested his leaving, even I had to admit that the house was more peaceful: no screaming matches when he'd come home drunk, no late night phone calls from the police, trying to be discreet by calling my father instead of hauling Marvin to jail. Once, when my mother had found marijuana in Marvin's coat, he reacted violently, pushing her against the wall before breaking down and apologizing. Though he remained at home until his next suspension from school, in a way, we all knew it was over then — my parents and Marvin had gone from hating themselves to hating each other, and there was no healing that. A few weeks after he left, I saw Marvin near the high school grounds. I could smell the funk of drugs on him, and it was all I could do to stop myself from asking if he'd been selling them, too. Instead, I just asked him when he was coming home.

"You get to thinking you're part of a family, that everything fits together," he told me. "But then you find out life comes down to the difference between what you believe about the world and what really is." Then he walked across the street, lit a cigarette, and kept going.

"I saw you," he says now. "When you guys robbed that place."

There is silence. I try a couple times to speak, but I can't form a word.

"What were you thinking?" Marvin asks. "There were police over there today. I saw them talking to the kids who are already back for school."

"It wasn't my fault," I say.

"I didn't say that. But I think we should talk about this."

"Not now," I say. I suddenly get the feeling that he is right outside, watching me again. I peek out the window, but there is nothing. Just heat, the end of August, dragonflies skimming near the surface of our pool.

"What? What do you have to do? I haven't talked to you in more than a year, and I don't want you to . . ." His voice trails off now, rising up at the end like an instrument running up the scale.

"Dad's coming," I say. I can't remember our entire childhood, but I'm almost positive this is the first time I've ever lied to my brother. It just comes out as instinct, the self-preservation of the guilty.

"Fine," he says, giving in. "This isn't over. We're going to talk about this. I want to meet you."

"I can't do that any time soon," I say. For years, I dreamed of things getting back to normal with my brother, clutching to that fantasy even after he'd moved out. But now, I've grown used to the idea that it will never be that way again — an idea that

55

Marvin helped put in my head — and I'm afraid that meeting Marvin will only reopen wounds, doing nothing to heal them.

"We'll figure something out," he says. He hangs up the phone without saying good-bye.

I put the picture back in Dad's drawer and then inspect the room to make sure that I haven't changed anything, feeling the need to cover my tracks.

It only takes a minute of being off the phone for the opposite impulse to kick in. Instead of being scared to talk to Marvin, all I really want to do is talk to him more, to ask him where he is, *who* he is, but I don't even have a number to call him back. I want to sit with him and learn about what his life is like now, how he makes it through, how I could help him. I think about the forty bucks in my back pocket and wonder how much Marvin could use it. I want to hear him turn up the radio and sing along like he used to, off-pitch and at the top of his lungs. I want to tell him about Lorrie, about how I'm learning the mysteries of another person. I want to tell him about how good the hoops team will be this season, about how I have a shot to start beside Jackson. I want to ask him for advice on how to deal with Branson, maybe have Marvin play big, protective brother like he did long ago. I want to hear him make fun of the teachers at the high school, make up dirty jokes about how Mrs. Marsh lost her middle finger.

Instead, I get in the car and head to the park. It's important that I get there in time to run the first game. It's important that we, the team, start that first game before anyone else can get the court. It's important that we stay together on these things.

Chapter 6

Everything is off. My shot, the team, everything. For the first two weeks of school we meet every day at the park to hoop, and it's all off. No flow, no rhythm, no pace to the games. Nothing.

It's been a string of problems: Saveen twists his ankle, not so bad as to cause missed time but bad enough to make him cautious, a fraction of the real Saveen; Trey gets it in his head he's the star of the court and starts jacking shots every trip down, inventing fouls if he misses, the game disintegrating into stoppages and silly arguments; turnovers become a contagion, like we've all forgotten how to dribble and pass, and instead of a squad that should win sectionals, we're beaten by five beer-bellied jerks off a local softball team, not once but three times, the last one with Saveen sitting out in disgust.

It's embarrassing. People from town actually come to the park during the evenings to play tennis or to grill out near the pavilion and take walks under the park lights, the afternoon traffic giving way to crickets and cicadas at dusk. These are some of the same townspeople who will be watching us under the gymnasium lights come November, and if our play now is any indication of future performances, I know I wouldn't be willing to pay the price of admission. Every time there's a particularly glaring mistake — a pass so wide of the mark it goes skimming into the grove of trees at the park's edge, or an air ball, some of them mine — I feel like the whole park stops to notice the disgrace of Cheneysburg's varsity. Coach Harper always preaches that good decision making creates good basketball, and for once I think there's some wisdom to what he says — guys are trying to make impossible passes through traffic, hoist jumpers from way beyond their range, go for steals they have no chance of getting. Bad decisions, all of them, and all of them turning our game to slop.

Some of it I attribute to Jackson's absence. He is the ignition for our team. Not just in the basics of hoops — demanding a quick outlet pass, pushing the ball up the floor, directing the offense — but in attitude, too. He's the one most likely to get chatter going on the floor, applaud good shots, encourage struggling players. Without Jackson we're out of sync at best — and completely incapable of functioning at worst. But he hasn't attended an after-school game yet, and when I see him in the hallways or in English class he gives me the same cool reception every time, an unenthused nod in my direction, his eyes already seeking an excuse not to talk to me. Lorrie quizzes me about Jackson's silence, but I dismiss it as an early-semester crunch in schoolwork. "His schedule's a killer," I say, "but he'll get used to it and all will be cool." Then I take her hand, trying to act natural, though things are so skewed I might just as well be holding on to her for balance.

Either way, Jackson's absence can't entirely explain the team's horrible play. He's been gone before — family vacations, his broken toe last year, the death of his uncle in the spring — and we've made out fine. Maybe a little bit ragged, but nothing this noticeable. There's something else affecting our play, and each day the tensions rise. The frustrations of Saveen and Trey are obvious, but even among the younger players there's a sense of strain, and rather than a congratulatory *Mighty* on the court, our games are soundtracked by curses of players angry at misplays.

Only Branson seems composed in the chaos. He seems to bully his way into the thick of the action, and he has always been a master at picking up garbage buckets off of loose balls and the confusion that ensues. Now, in the first weeks of September, he usually scores more than Saveen, and I barely get a look at the hoop anymore. From our last games of the summer the flow of play couldn't be more different.

We keep playing, though, and tonight I'm squeezing in one last game before a date with Lorrie. She's at the court, too, watching us finish before I catch a ride home with her to clean up for the evening. I can't handle having her see us play so poorly, so I work a little harder and finally pop myself loose from Branson, open for a fifteen-footer on the baseline. Only the kid who's trying to handle the rock misses me by about six feet. Turnover. Again.

"Jesus," I say. "Put the ball *here*." I put my hands out in his direction in the ready position, pump them a couple times for emphasis.

"Easy on the boy," Branson says. "Can't every pass be perfect."

"You just love this, don't you?" I say. "You like it that we can't even play anymore. That way you can be in charge."

"Easy," he says again. He smiles, though, enjoying my anger. "It's off-season play, Nate. Plenty of time to work the kinks out, bro."

I start back downcourt, getting ready to guard Branson. "I'm not your bro," I say under my breath.

Branson arrives where I'm standing and pivots hard, his hip colliding with me, his right elbow up near my chin. "What's that, Nate? You say something?"

I push back, getting low for leverage as I edge him out of position. "I said, don't act like everything's cool." There are times I still thrill at the outlaw quality of our theft, but with our poor play and the knowledge that Marvin witnessed us I can't pretend like the danger doesn't scare me.

"Thought you were a team player, Nate. Couldn't be you're just out for your own like everyone else?" He flares out to the perimeter, claps his hands once to demand the ball.

I get up into him, tight, almost chest-to-chest. "I'm not like you," I say. "Son of a bitch." The ball swings to the opposite side and I know I should sink into the lane and away from Branson to play help-side, but I stick right with him, my elbow planted under his ribs.

"Watch your mouth," he says. He starts to uproot me, push his way into the lane. He jabs hard into the lane and gets his hands in on me for leverage. "You think your honey over there would want to know her boy's just a piece-of-shit thief like everyone else?" Then he shoves me across the lane and flares quickly back out to the wing, calling for the ball.

I see them start to swing it to him, and I sprint toward Branson, glide past a screen without breaking stride, and — there it is; my timing missing for weeks is rediscovered in a flash — I arrive with the ball, tap it away with my right hand, scoop it cleanly with my left, and push downcourt ahead of everyone, lungs burning with effort. Two dribbles and I'm at the hoop, rising effortlessly to lay it in, and I can feel myself lifting away from the baggage that's been holding me down.

Then Branson makes contact.

One elbow finds my skull and the other catches me just below my right shoulder, both of them throwing me down. There is weightlessness for a moment, my feet parallel with my head, and then it's just the ground rushing up to meet me.

More than feeling the contact, I hear it. A crunch of my shoulders on blacktop and then some pops in my back as my own weight contorts over me, the pressure rising up my spine. I try to reach for balance with my hands, but I feel myself flip over and then land again, this time flat on my stomach, my wind knocked clean out.

I lie still and take inventory of my parts. Hands, check. Feet, check. Then I try moving. Wrists, elbows, knees, and neck, check. Through a thick buzz I can hear the voices argue — what sounds like Branson's voice knifes through the fog toward me, but the words are unintelligible. I try to get up, but there's a hand on my shoulder, pinning me down. I try to slap it away, but it's locked firmly at the elbow, unshakable. I think it's Branson coming after me for more, but then I see that the hand is attached to Saveen, who is just guarding me for protection, his other hand cautioning everyone else away.

"Easy, Nate," he says. "Easy, baby."

On the other end of Saveen is Branson, still making noise. Convinced he has me under control, Saveen turns toward Branson and pushes him back a few feet — not hard or violent, but enough to settle him.

"That's enough," he says. "Everyone, that's enough. Let's call it until Monday. We'll come back and get at it then."

"Ain't gonna be no change by Monday," somebody says.

The group starts to disperse, but Branson lingers. He gets up to Saveen's face. "You're in this, too, boy," he says. "Don't be trying to play daddy to these guys when you're in it, too." Then he looks down at me. "And, hey, I'm sorry the kid can't handle himself, but that was a clean play and you know it."

"I know," Saveen says.

Branson leaves, and for the first time I see that Lorrie is also crouched beside me. I stand, but my legs are still rubbery, my head all fog. I can feel abrasions on my elbows and the heels of my hands, like small bites.

"Why did you say that was clean?" Lorrie asks Saveen. "Branson could have killed him."

Saveen shrugs his huge shoulders. "It's best not to fight Branson."

"What?" Lorrie's angry, her eyes like lasers, chin out. I've seen this look in her before, after a lecture from her mother or a cruel remark by someone at school, and I've always been thankful Lorrie's anger was never directed at me. "You're freaking nine feet tall, Saveen. And you can't stand up to Branson?"

"It's not that," he says. "It's . . ."

Lorrie pulls me away from Saveen, both hands wrapped hot on my arm. "Forget it, Saveen. Jesus, be a man. Be the guy that people expect you to be."

Lorrie helps me to the car, asking me repeatedly if I'm okay. I continue saying yes, but with every step I discover a new pain — one in my ankle, my chin, my collarbone, a few in my chest and stomach that feel like something in my core has been punctured. But my breathing is coming easier, and I climb into the car on my own. Before Lorrie starts the engine, though, I see Saveen at my window.

"You gonna be okay, Nate?" he says.

"I think so," I say. I give Saveen a wink, trying to look sure of myself. "Did I make the bucket?"

"Jesus, man. Mighty. Asking about the goddamn shot. Hell, yes, you made it." He reaches in the window then and puts his massive hand on my arm. "I'm sorry. Maybe I should have knocked Branson on his ass, but I'm just trying to hold this team together."

"I know," I say.

From the other side Lorrie leans over, still hot. "Oh, sure. Now you're going to be best friends with him. Good timing, Saveen."

Saveen looks down, spits on the ground. Behind him I can see the park, which has been bustling the whole time. In the confusion I'd forgotten about our constant audience, and I wonder what they saw, what they heard. "Can you talk to Jackson?" Saveen asks. "We sure as hell need his ass here."

"Tell me."

I can feel the soreness setting; I can sense where the bruises and knots will be. The pool is soothing, bracingly cold as September settles over it, and I swing my arm beneath the water, testing its range of motion.

"Tell me."

"Stop it," I say. The sun is putting itself down behind Lorrie, who sits at the edge of the pool in T-shirt and shorts, dangling her legs in the water. I want to just drift, listen to the water lap the sides of the pool, let the world grow dark around the two of us until tomorrow. "It's nothing."

"I'm not stupid, Nate. I play basketball, and I've seen a million games. What Branson did to you is never about nothing."

"How's your team looking?" I ask.

"Great. I'm shooting the ball well. We're the best team in

the county, easy. Now," she slaps her hand on the tile, "quit stalling and tell me."

I swim to her, push myself up to sit on the side, the water rolling off me. I look at her, but there's something different. She's the same person, of course: jet-black hair pulled back, eyes intent and wide, a scar above her lip — a childhood bike accident — so small that it almost escapes vision. But the fragility, the delicate look of fine china she always had, is replaced by a suggestion of a full-blown adult inside her, toughened by responsibility. Determination is set in the corners of her mouth, worry pinching tension into her temples.

It catches me unaware, and it takes me a moment to begin answering her question. Lorrie puts her hand on my thigh. "Whatever it is," she says, "you can tell me. Anything."

It's not the first time I've noticed a change in Lorrie. The first one came years ago: We were at the pool then, too, and my other friends had scattered for home and dinner and chores and television. Lorrie remained, springing high off the board in repetition, as if she thought she might disprove the laws of gravity and soar to heights of her own choosing, and I sat on the steps toweling myself silently and slowly realizing, like someone discovering loose change is made of solid gold, that Lorrie was not the little girl who always wanted to roughhouse with the boys, not the girl who wanted to race to the corner, not the girl of a runny nose and skinned elbows and holes forever tearing in the knees of her brand-new blue jeans. No. She was Lorrie McIntyre, a full-blown teenager, and she was in her bathing suit at my pool, alone with me. It nearly left me breathless, just as the sight of her now — tan and wet beside me — makes my heart race. I consider taking her hand and leading her inside, trying to distract her in a far more appealing way than discussing basketball.

"Nate." Her voice is soft, pleading.

Finally, I start speaking. And once I start, it's a stream of words. It starts with Branson — his menace, his power, my fear — and it ends with him, too — him crushing me to the ground only an hour ago. As I tell the story, I try to centralize Branson in the events, stress that none of it would have happened without him and that I was merely standing to the side, caught up like an innocent in his wake. But as I tell it I keep stumbling over the part when Jackson leaves, his jaw tensed as he drives away, the gravel at the Sigma Chi court ricocheting off his wheel wells. That's the hard part to tell Lorrie, because it's so clear that Jackson was strong enough to resist Branson's pull, smart enough to trust his own mind, and because there's no separating the moment I stood there on the court, hearing the hiss of Jackson's wheels grow fainter on the road, and the moments in school when he is an impenetrable wall of silence. But I get through it, explain the risks, the foundation of the team already crumbling beneath the strain of the last few weeks.

"It's Branson," I find myself saying. "He's orchestrating this whole thing. And anyone who challenges him ends up like I did today. Flattened. It's him." But the words sound phony even to me, and I don't see how Lorrie can do anything but hate me for saying it.

I wait for Lorrie's special brand of anger — a mix of her father's red-faced volume and her mother's shaming disappointment — to finally target me. I look at her after staring down at the pool the whole time I've been talking, expecting those embers in her eyes. Instead they are steady and dark like wet stones.

Lorrie purses her lips and exhales, almost a whistle. "That's a lot to deal with," she says. She kicks her leg once in the water, then raises it and seems to study the water streaming off. Calm. "Do you think you can get away with it?" she asks.

"I don't know. Nobody's cracked yet, far as I know. And it's been two weeks."

"So nobody saw you?"

I almost answer *no* without thinking, so focused on shaping the events to absolve myself that I've edited out Marvin.

"Just one person," I say.

I must be smiling, because Lorrie says, "That's not funny, Nate."

I shake my head. "No. I don't mean that. I mean it's kind of amazing really. The only person who saw us is Marvin."

"Your brother?"

"Yes. Marvin. My brother."

Lorrie purses her lips again, lets go a full whistle this time. Then we're both silent. She moves closer, puts her hand on mine, like we're huddling beneath the knowledge we now share. Inside I hear a door close. I realize that I'm hungry, that we haven't eaten. And then the dings and aches of my body start ringing their various bells, make me conscious of my body again.

"He hasn't said anything to anybody except me. But he said the police have been coming by the frat."

"You've been talking to him?"

"Just once."

She squeezes my hand. "Then I guess we should go see him."

I'm surprised at her lack of hesitation. Even for Lorrie, suggesting we go see Marvin is direct. She doesn't blink, though, just presses her fingers deeper into my hand. I try to imagine seeing Marvin again, and it almost makes me flinch — not because I'm scared to do it, but because it's hard to even picture. All I have to go on are the memories of our last few meetings, all of them awkward. At the same time, though, I know I have to do it. I can feel Lorrie's hands massage mine, almost pressing in the realization that I can't avoid Marvin any longer.

Chapter 7

The most dismaying thing — more than the theft, more than being called on it by Marvin — is that I have to *ask* somebody to find my own brother. I know the general vicinity, of course, but our family is so fractured that to meet Marvin my only choices are to go door-to-door in the shady complexes near the fraternities until I find his place, or to admit my ignorance and ask. So I choose the latter, shelving my pride to ask a senior, one of the stoners who I know once hung out with Marvin, if he knows the exact apartment. He tells me, though I can see follow-up questions almost written on his face: *Why do you even have to ask? What do you want from Marvin, anyway? Is this Gilman brother turning out just like the one before him?* I take off before he can actually say any of it out loud. It isn't pleasant, but it gets me the information I need. For the visit itself, though, I need Lorrie along for support.

Marvin's place possesses a certain pulse from its squalor, the opposite of how my mother keeps our house immaculately clean and lifeless. In the stairway to his apartment the bulb was burned out, but in the darkness I could hear moths and flies flitting against the walls, my hand picking up bits of cobweb from the railing. Inside I can hear the drip of a faucet, the hyper thrum of an old refrigerator, songs battling fuzz on his radio's reception. There are a variety of smells fighting one another: burnt toast; incense spiraling at the foot of Marvin's chair; a pile of rumpled and acrid clothes behind a stereo speaker; the stale cigarettes in the ashtray overflowing onto a plate; and another unnamed smell lurking beneath all of it, something dodgy and slightly rotten.

I expected Lorrie to be the one on-edge in this visit, but she has already found a seat, her legs crossed elegantly. She could be at an honors banquet. Marvin keeps fiddling with his lighter like he's debating the pros and cons of another cigarette. Nobody is speaking. I walk to the window in Marvin's living room — I guess there's nothing else to call it since it's not the kitchen, with the crumbs and streaks of dirt on the linoleum, and it's not his bedroom, a square little cell made to look smaller by the clothes and discs and magazines sprawled on the floor. I peek out, my finger bringing up a layer of dust as I part the blinds. Sure enough, it's a perfect view of the Sigma Chi court, which is almost vacant now except for two frat boys sitting at the back door and passing a bottle, tipping it to their mouths in the light's mellow glow.

"Sit down, Nate." It's Lorrie, taking control.

I do as she says, plopping beside her on Marvin's futon. I immediately want to stand again, pace away the nerves.

"Hey, Nate," Marvin says.

"Hi, Marvin." It's about the tenth time we've said hi to each other, like we're trying out our names again, casting them like nets into the ocean of memory, seeing what we can reel in. Despite his apartment's mess, Marvin looks well put together, far better than he looked the last time I saw him. His clothes are clean, even if his T-shirt is wrinkled, and his eyes are bright and alert. There's more flesh on his face than I remember. More flesh everywhere, and if it weren't for those eyes I remember from childhood — still a hint of that mischief from ferreting out my dad's dirty magazines from deep in the closet — he'd look like a full-grown man. He has my father's broad forehead, just without the groove-deep wrinkles, and my mother's thin lips, two perfectly straight slices across his face. His hair is cut short, not the mangy curls and tangles he let grow out after first leaving the house, and it's still wet from a shower, making it look ink black before it dries into a deep brown the same shade as mine.

Lorrie uncrosses her legs and leans forward. "Marvin, it's been a long time since those old pool parties." She puts an apologetic look on her face — like her mother getting ready to ask questions about school. "But there are some things we need to talk about right now." I almost double-take, wondering who she is, so calm in this situation, like she's negotiating a contract signing.

"I know," Marvin says. "About a million things."

"Nate told me about how you saw what happened across the street. With the team."

Even if I'm unnerved by her taking the reins, I'm glad she's doing the talking — it saves me from having to come up with anything. Here he is: Marvin, my brother. And damn if it's the last thing I want, but the images come rushing back at me: my brother shuffling from the Hartwells' house five summers ago, blinking in the sun's glare; cries for help ringing from Mr. Gaston's mouth as he leads Marvin out; Ray Hartwell stooping to set the basketball down on the driveway before running toward them, stopping when he gets to Marvin, both of them looking down at Marvin's white T-shirt splotched in a deep, foreboding crimson. My brother's face. I watched that happen.

"Nate, you want to talk about that?" Marvin nods toward the window, toward the frat.

"There was nothing I could do," I say. "I would change it if I could."

"I know," Marvin says. He looks down at his hands. "But now that it's done, we've got to deal with it. I mean, there are some seriously pissed-off people across the street, and they have cops coming by here almost every day. They've been asking people that live near here for tips."

"Have they come here?" Lorrie asks.

"No," Marvin says. "One thing we have going is that Cheneysburg cops are never in much of a hurry. But they *will* get around to it." There's a deep change in the pitch of the refrigerator's hum, like a car shifting gears, and Marvin excuses himself to the kitchen. While we hear Marvin mutter over deep thuds, Lorrie looks at me with a glare. Now she's got the smolder going.

"What?" I ask.

"Will you *talk*? You sit there like nothing happened."

"Sorry," I say. "Not exactly the easiest conversation, Lorrie."

"I'm sorry," she says. The refrigerator returns to its previous tone, and Lorrie puts her hand on my knee, squeezes. "Just try."

Marvin sits again, and there is sweat beading at his temples. He shakes a cigarette loose — no hesitation now. He puts the lighter to it and puffs with a look of deep and meaningful satisfaction.

"So, little brother," he says. He smiles then, a strange cockiness coming to his face, the look he'd get when we played one-on-one and he knew he was getting the better of me. "What's your plan? What are you gonna do?"

I can feel Lorrie looking at me, waiting for me to answer. "Jesus," I say. "I don't know. I mean, there's not much I can do now."

"So you're not going to come clean?" Marvin asks.

"To who? The cops?"

"Sure. Or the guys across the street. The ones you stole from. It might be best that way."

I feel a slight squeeze from Lorrie, what I guess is an encouragement to do the right thing. I don't answer, though. Marvin taps the ash from his cigarette and leans forward for emphasis.

"It's going to be a lot of guilt to carry around," he says. "I know it's hard to own up to something like that, but in the end it might be harder not to." He looks to the side of the room, like he's distracted by some sudden movement. "Trust me. Your conscience will be worse than the punishment."

I look to Lorrie for advice, but she just stares right back at me without even blinking — it's my life, I suppose, and I can't expect my girlfriend to answer questions for me. But I know what she'd do. She'd tell the truth. But then, she wouldn't have robbed a frat to begin with.

"It won't change anything," I say.

"You say that now."

"I can't do it." There's a shameful feeling in my gut, hunger and nausea both at once.

Marvin stands, picks up the ashtray and the dish next to it, takes them to the garbage can, and clatters them empty. He comes back and sits, smoking still, trying to look nonchalant. "Fine," he says. "I mean, I guess that's what I expected. You've got to save your own ass."

"It's not just me," I shout. It's a surprise to hear my voice at such volume. "It's the whole team, our whole season. If it were only me then maybe I'd say something, but now I'd be selling out my teammates — Saveen, Luke, Trey." I start to tick them off on my fingers but stop when I realize the next name belongs to Branson.

"That's true," Lorrie says, surprising me.

There's a long silence then, and Marvin's eyes drift around the room; the edge they had a few minutes ago vanishes, replaced by a lost and vacant look, like he's alone, trying to make sense of a memory or a dream. Outside, a car door slams. A bottle breaks. There are shouts from the frat, the high squeals of girls arriving.

"It's a small town," Marvin says. "There's a damn good chance you'll get caught anyway. If you admit it before they

74

catch you, you might get some pity. Maybe forgiveness. Otherwise, this town can hold a grudge. Goddamn this town."

"Are you going to tell what you saw?" Lorrie asks. "If the police come here and ask you, will you tell?"

Marvin gives her a withering look, his jaw cocked a little to one side. There's the fatigue, the pain. His hair might be cut short and he may have gained some muscle, but he can't gloss over that defeated look he's carried around town for the last few years. He hangs his head, chin almost to chest, then looks back up at us with his eyes thinned. "I don't figure I owe them a goddamn thing. I really don't. Nate's secret is safe with me." He leans back in his chair, its feet hovering an inch off the floor; then he swings one thick leg across the other and brings his chair back down with a thud. He waves a cloud of smoke away from his face. "Anyway. I suppose that's that."

As if nothing happened, Marvin starts quizzing me about my life, about school and hoops. Questions pepper me and Lorrie: Have we thought about college? Are there any good scandals among the school faculty? Do kids still go to the old haunts — Bethel Bridge, Four Arches, Pine Hill Cemetery — to scare the bejesus out of freshmen? He knows Lorrie and I have been dating for some time, says he could see that one coming from about the time he was ten. He knows she plays hoops, too, and knows that both our teams have promise for the coming year. I'm surprised how much he knows, and when I say so, Marvin tells me you can learn a lot once you start paying attention to the place where you live.

75

"Plus I got those," he says. He points to a stack of newspapers from Lafayette stacked in a blue milk crate by the garbage can. "The fraternity actually gets a few delivered, but since nobody over there is up before ten in the morning, I usually help myself to one of them." He pauses and smiles. "I don't think they'll miss those as much as they do their stereos."

He's the only one who laughs at his joke. Lorrie frowns and says we should go. She says she has to be home soon, which is true, but I can tell there's something else bothering her. It's as if we were here only to discuss the terms of secrecy, the cost attached to it, and any conversation beyond that — and the familiarity Marvin shows — is a waste of her time.

Marvin blusters to the door and opens it for us, stammering out a thank-you for the visit. The departure is as clumsy as our arrival, and it's like we didn't come at all — a chasm reopening between me and Marvin, our relationship precarious as ever, Lorrie leading me forward.

We're back in the darkness of the stairwell, the night air smelling clean through the screen door at the bottom of the stairs. I can hear more people gathering at the fraternity, the self-pitying whine of college rock coming from their cars, their clamor always invading.

"Nate." It's Marvin, at the top of the stairs, his frame cutting a silhouette against the light of his doorway. He says my name with urgency, but then I see his shoulders drop into a more casual stance. "You know, whatever you decide is cool with me."

"Thanks," I say.

"All I'm saying is, you know, you can come visit whenever you want. We don't have to talk about all that other stuff."

Marvin disappears behind his door. "I will," I say, but there's no way of knowing if he hears me.

Then we're outside, my face flushing in the night as we pass by Sigma Chi on our way to Lorrie's car. I hear someone say "*Cheneysburg, Indi-fucking-ana*" in a long, drawn-out tone, the rest of them laughing like it's a punch line.

"Your brother," Lorrie says. "Wow." She rolls her eyes, takes another bite of her cheeseburger.

It's nine now, and we're just eating, both of us scarfing greasy burgers and burnt fries as fast and impolite as stray dogs. Some date. There are only a few other people in the place: two workers back in the kitchen gossiping — I can hear the woman say *no waaaay* every so often — one worker mopping forlornly out front; a fifty-something in a suit staring out the window as he sips his milk shake, looking borderline suicidal; a drunk college student crouched in a booth, on the verge of passing out.

"What do you mean?" I ask. There is a tone in her words, one I can't quite place.

"I don't mean it that way," she says.

"What way?"

"Well, it was a shock, that's all." She returns to her meal, shaking her head. "It's nothing."

I'm too tired to argue with her after all that's happened today. Still, there's that tone, an itch I can't reach. Lorrie, who I thought I knew so well, has become pure mystery.

I see the cashier shut down his register, then nod toward the worker behind the mop, who walks to the door and flips the *Closed* sign to the outside world, pinches the tiny switch on the sign's cord, extinguishing its neon. There is an unnatural noise from the college boy — the *pinhead*, as Branson would call him — a sound that seems to bubble from some marsh inside of him.

"Let's go home," Lorrie says. "You look awful."

"Not as bad as the rest of the people in here," I say. She laughs, and so I point to the college drunk. "You didn't tell me your other boyfriend would be here." Lorrie elbows me, trying to act like she's offended. "And your sugar daddy," I say, pointing toward the man in the suit.

"Stop it," she says. "How can you be joking now?"

But she's smiling at me and hooks her arm around mine. I'm still confused by her, but I remind myself that she could have given up on me as soon as I told her about Sigma Chi, and as we leave, the worker unlocking the door and then relocking it behind us with a clunk of the bolt, I wonder what Lorrie's privately thinking about me, if the picture of me in her head has also altered.

When we get to my driveway, I can see the dull glow of the television. There is a small, cruel urge to walk inside and wake my parents, tell them everything about the day, watch the bomb go off in their faces. I lean over and kiss Lorrie. There is a moment of hesitation on her end, though. Or perhaps I just imagine that.

"Lorrie," I say. She looks straight ahead, like she's still driving, keeping a safe distance from the car ahead. "I'm sorry."

"Don't," she says. "Don't apologize. Things happen."

"You're not mad?"

She puts her hand on my thigh and turns to look at me, a strange expression curled on her face. Again she looks older, like she's leaped ahead of me in age and is looking back through time's telescope, waiting for me to catch up. "I don't know," she says. "It's not *mad*. That's not what I feel."

"Then what?"

"Stop," she says. She pats my hand and shakes her head. "That's just it. If I could tell you I would, but it's not like there's some easy word for it. I have to figure it out. Everything's just kind of changing."

I start to talk again, but I don't even know what to ask. She puts her finger to my lips, a short and soft connection. "Good night, Nate," she says.

I get to my room so fast it's like the rest of the house doesn't exist. I try to picture Marvin across town, wonder if he's resting in the tangle of his sheets, the mattress thrown on the floor like a raft on water, or he's out in the night, making noise behind the mysterious walls of Moore's Pub or cruising through alleys seeking vice, looking cool and mean, cigarette pinched in the corner of his mouth. I drift toward sleep wondering if it's possible to ever really know another person.

Chapter 8

Like Marvin, the town gets its real news from Lafayette, though they only cover anything in Cheneysburg once or twice a year. The local weekly, *The Cheneysburg Gazette*, purports to serve up local news every Monday, but it's mostly a week-in-review, stories cobbled together from other papers over the weekend, plus a calendar of events for the town: bingo games, arts and crafts sales, athletic events. Then there are the letters to the editor, the complaints and suggestions, or once in a while a guest column by the mayor, Dad's pal. If there's ever any real news — and even that's a stretch — it's about road improvements or store openings. When the county fair comes around, they cover it like it's the Olympics. It also takes ages for anything to actually make the paper, so some days — like today — they cover something that's almost a month old.

I'm forced into reading it by the social studies staff, which always uses the *Gazette* for current events, this year from Mr. Davies, who seems about as unenthused by the paper as we are. This morning I'm also quizzed on the *Gazette* before I even get to school. Over breakfast, my dad paused over the paper. He grunted, put his spoon back in his bowl like an afterthought. Then he folded the paper on itself so only the article of interest was visible, a great rustling and wrinkling of the edges disturbing our usual breakfast silence.

"You know anything about this?" he asked.

I looked at the headline: **LOCAL FRATERNITY BURGLED — LOOTERS STILL AT LARGE**. My impulse was actually to laugh — first Branson called what we did *liberating* and now the paper refers to it with *burgled*. Neither of those seems close to accurate — though I'm not sure what words I'd use if I had to write the headline — and it makes it seem like an event that happened in an entirely different town or something wholly unreal, like it's a teaser for some network movie. But I knew enough to stifle laughter; I knew that wasn't the message I wanted to send — I've already made the mistake of piquing my parents' curiosity, courtesy of my bruises from the run-in with Branson. I played them off as battle scars that go with the territory — "Anybody says basketball's a noncontact sport lies," I said — but I saw their doubt register, brows furrowing in concern. At the breakfast table this morning, I sensed the same doubt, and in some strange way, it was as if they were more alive than they'd been in years, using all their senses at last.

"Well?" my father said. My mother had shoved herself off the counter, hovering over my shoulder.

I pulled the paper close to me and pretended to read it, though I was sure I knew more than any newspaper hack could.

Then I looked back up at him. "No," I said. "Why?" I thought it came out as convincing, pure indifference, but I saw his eyes narrow.

"Isn't that the place you boys play ball?"

"Well, yeah. But we haven't been there in weeks. I didn't see anything while we were there."

He jerked the paper back and reread the article, looking at me once in a while across the table. My mother sighed and said she was going to go lie down. That was all there was to it, but I got the feeling of having a hook snagged in my skin and not knowing how much slack was on the line before it would bite deep into flesh and muscle, reeling me.

Now, at school, it's a similar routine with Mr. Davies. Only while he's focusing on an editorial about the mayor giving tax abatements to a local company, I finally take time to read the entire article. What they know, according to the police: an inventory of what was stolen, including unique and identifiable possessions; a general time frame for the burglary — between August 19, when a frat member made a stopover at the house on a trip to Milwaukee, and August 25, when the first members started to move back in for school — a loose count of the number involved, perhaps "upward of five or six," the sheriff thinks, based on how much was taken; and a guess of the vehicle used — large, probably a van — to haul off the loot. But the bit they don't know outweighs all of that: They have no clue who did it. There are no witnesses. ("At least none that have piped up," says the sheriff.) There were signs of damage at one of the outside doors, but the members admit that the lock has been broken for years. Otherwise there are no signs of forced entry, which leads police to consider the job the work of people who know the fraternity well. Theories include a rival frat, a connection to a string of similar thefts stretching from Lafayette to Louisville, disgruntled university employees, and any number of local juveniles. As I read, I feel distanced from the event, and even though I know the last theory is the right one, I find myself caught up in the rival fraternity premise — it almost makes more sense to me than what actually happened. I try to imagine a history in which all crime in Cheneysburg is tagged on the college boys and I'm innocent of everything but a deadly long-range jump shot.

"What are your thoughts, Nathan?" It's Mr. Davies, in front of the classroom, pinching the chalk between his finger and thumb so hard he grinds white dust onto his hand.

"I don't know," I say.

Mr. Davies is disappointed, I can tell. That's an answer he expects from other students, but he counts on me to contribute some kind of opinion on whatever topic we're discussing.

"You're not even on the same page, are you?" He walks toward me, and I try to find the right page, looking at neighboring desks to try to catch up. I can feel eyes on me, hear people starting to murmur. "What are you reading? That article about the fraternity?"

"No," I say. "We were talking about that thing with the mayor."

He pauses at my desk, frowning. He knows. Who else

knows? My parents? Coach Harper? The whole class? The cops? My throat tightens with paranoia. I can feel my nerves falter, the free-throw shooter choking in crunch time.

"Yes," Mr. Davies says. "I suppose we *were* talking about that." He backs off, looks to the rest of the class. "Anybody else have thoughts on that, since Mr. Gilman seems a bit lost today?"

There's snickering in the classroom, people taking pleasure in the A student getting called out by the teacher. Then there's Lorrie's voice: "I think if the companies are growing and helping people get jobs, it makes sense to help them." Her voice is cool, the way it's been on the phone the last few days. "Unless, of course, the companies don't do what they say," she adds. I can't be sure, but I think I see her glance at me with those final words.

I catch up to her in the hallway after class, and I ask her if she read the article on Sigma Chi.

"Of course," she says. "I'm pretty sure everybody did."

"Does it sound bad?" I say.

"It doesn't sound good." She looks down, picks at her notebook with her nails. "But then I already know the truth. I don't know how it would look if I didn't know."

We hold hands and walk down the hall, trying to give the appearance that nothing has changed, but I can tell from her touch that things are different. Her hand is just kind of there, a place holder. She seems as absentminded about it as if she were holding a leash. The hallway is the same. There's laughter and loud talk, the slamming of lockers, people sighing as they heave bookbags to their shoulders, the creak of the bathroom door aching open and shut, a freshman at the door who's been bullied into standing sentry for the smokers inside. I tell myself that none of them care, that the worry about being found out is just in my head, and as I watch the school go about its Monday morning without even pausing to look at Lorrie and me I think that might be true. Only ahead I see Branson, Saveen, and Luke in a small huddle, heads bent down as they talk.

"Your cohorts," Lorrie says.

I remember just days ago feeling delicious wickedness over what we'd done, the special bond I felt with Saveen when he gave me that scheming wink. There's none of that now, and I hate myself for giving in to it at all.

"Don't," I say. I pull Lorrie off to the side, take both her hands. "I told you I'm sorry. I never meant for that stuff to happen."

"I'm just teasing," she says. "Don't get mad at *me*."

We start to walk again, and we reach the spot where we break off — Lorrie to choir and me to biology. "That look back in Mr. Davies' class, though. Did I just imagine that? You looked angry."

"God, Nate." She puts her hand on my hip, playful. "I'm not allowed to look at my boyfriend during class? I mean, I would like to be able to go on as if this had never happened." She tells me to come over tonight, just like everything is normal, then turns toward class, her hair flipping across her shoulders. She turns back with a little wave — *bye-bye*, she mouths.

At the court, it's the same old, only worse. Branson has focused his aggression on the younger players now — elbows, not-so-subtle hip checks — and they back down immediately, some of them even throwing their hands in the air in surrender. Saveen dishes some back to Branson, though, giving him a solid foul on a drive. The two of them square off, chests puffed, and for a moment it looks like they're going to throw. But Branson just gives a sneer and scoops up the ball. "Check it," he says, and we resume.

I call for a sub and take a seat next to Trey, who's also taking a breather. We sit on top of a picnic table that borders the court, the wood soft and bowed. In the summer, it would hold so much heat it would burn us through our shorts, but now it's cold, the chill setting in on us while we're resting. I lean back and dig my fingers into the wood, try to pry up a large, satisfying splinter with my nails. If only we would have made this our regular court during the summer, we could have avoided all our trouble. But no, the fraternity court always seemed more exclusive to us, a place we could think of as ours.

"Man," Trey says. He swings his head toward me, a beaten-dog look on it, hair hanging down in his eyes. He'll have to get it cut for Coach Harper before the season starts.

"What?" I ask.

"Fuck this."

That seems to just about sum it up, and I nod and blink

sweat from my eyes. But I hear the thump of a basketball from across the parking lot, the skid of a sneaker across dirty pavement. I look up: Jackson. At Saveen's request, I'd called Jackson over the weekend, but got no reply. I stand on the bench and wave to him, slap Trey on the shoulder, and point, like Jackson's a long-awaited ship arriving to shore. "Jackson," we both call to him.

He just nods, though, keeps approaching at a leisurely pace, crossing the ball between his legs with each stride. On the court, the action slows as a few players rubberneck to check him out, but the game keeps going in a jerking, distracted flow.

"You come to run?" Trey says.

Jackson tucks the ball in the crook of his arm. "I can do that."

"Mighty," Trey says. He puts his fist out, meets Jackson's. Then Jackson turns to me and does the same.

"We got next, boys," Trey calls to the court, then sprints over to the water fountain at the edge of the tennis courts.

Jackson takes Trey's place beside me, his foot bouncing off the bench so fast it's almost like he's picking up a rhythm that's coming from the core of the wood. He spins the ball skyward in mock jump shots, lets it fall right back to his hands.

"We cool, Jackson?" I say.

He doesn't look at me. "You saw the article in the paper, right?"

I nod. "You?"

Jackson looks at me with a sullen stare. "Damn, man. You think there's anybody who didn't read that?" He puts the ball in his lap, his foot ceasing its rhythm. "Coach saw it."

"I figured that might happen." I turn to him. "Look, Jackson. I'm sorry."

He looks away, shaking his head. "Save it. If we want to have a decent season, I figure I need to start practicing with you guys. Thing is, Coach isn't exactly happy about that article."

He squints at the sun, which is starting to dip behind the huge tulip trees surrounding the park. Farther out, the water tower's side is starting to glow with evening sun, like a crescent moon. It's only seven and already near dark, the fall starting to rear its head.

"He's gonna call us all into his office tomorrow," Jackson continues. "I found out from Tuman."

"Tuman the equipment manager?"

"Yeah. He heard Coach talking to the assistants and asked me what I knew. I didn't say anything."

"But you talk to the equipment manager?"

Jackson looks at me again, that same stare: part disapproval, part pity. "Nate, you're a smart guy. And you're still my friend. But sometimes you don't get it."

It's time for the next game to roll and Jackson and I are on, so I don't get a chance to ask him what that means. Except I'm not even sure to how to ask — it seems like by asking I'd only draw another stare.

I walk to the court, feeling a little tentative, but Jackson dribbles — behind his back, around and between his legs, crossovers quick as a blink — like this day's no different from any other. A few guys pat him on the shoulder to welcome him back. Then Branson swaggers up, brushing into me as he walks past.

"So you're not too good for us anymore?" Branson says.

"Never said I was," Jackson says. He doesn't even look at Branson, just keeps dribbling with his eyes on the bucket at the far end of the court.

"Well, don't expect us to throw a party for you," Branson says. He reaches out and squeezes Jackson's shoulder, hard. "But it's cool to have you back."

"Let's just play," Jackson says.

We run, and it's not like everything clicks right back into place. Even Jackson seems a step off-pace — he just misses a steal in the passing lane; one of his feeds to Saveen comes in low, banging off his shin; he lets a lowly freshman get past him for a bucket. The whole game is still a bit ragged in general, and I find myself staying passive, just reversing the ball unless I'm wide open. But we keep running, and even if Saveen isn't getting dime after dime from Jackson, I can see some of his confidence back: He swats away a shot on one end and then sprints to the other, leaping to catch a pass on the break and laying it in on the reverse side all without coming down. We start to find a tempo, even if we miss a beat now and then, and with the air cooling I feel like I could run ten games in a row. Later I pop loose on the wing and Jackson hits me right in time. I let fly and bury the J.

Jogging back, I extend my fist to Jackson. He just nods at me, though. "Good shot," he says. "Now D up."

As the game winds down, though, we return to our misplays, and Branson keeps things tangled and rough on the inside, ending it all on a junk lay-in off a loose ball. There were probably about seven fouls on the play, but there are no whistles on the playground. So that's it. Game over. Despite Jackson's return, Branson wins again.

But there was a glimmer, just the smallest of sparks, and that's enough to build on.

I roll up my car to Jackson, who's walking home. "Ride?"

"Naw, man. I'm hoofing it."

"We cool?"

"I told you, save it. It's okay."

He turns then, heads up the hill to cut through the pavilion at the west edge of the park. I hook my car around in the opposite direction, flicking my lights on in the waning daylight.

At Lorrie's I get yet another quiz about the article in the paper, this one from her father. Like my dad, he knows we play at Sigma Chi during the summers.

"Looks like your court had a few problems there, Nate," he says. His hand is on my shoulder, rocking me back and forth. It bothers me as much as ever, but I don't let it show — I know if he's still roughhousing with me then he must think everything's okay. Mrs. McIntyre is minding her own business, cleaning up after dinner, but I can see her throw a worried glance our way now and then. Lorrie is off in the family room, picking out a movie for us to watch. Everyone plays their normal roles.

Mr. McIntyre puts enough weight on my shoulder to get me to sit down at the kitchen table; then he sits next to me, stroking his chin with his thumb and finger, like he's deep in thought. He looks at me, trying to put on a serious face, his lower lip pushed out slightly. "You don't know anything about that stuff at the frat, do you, Nate?"

I put my hands up in protest, acting as if I'm shocked he'd even have to ask. I know this routine will go over with Mr. McIntyre, an eternal optimist, especially when it comes to the basketball team. "No way, sir," I say.

Lorrie must have overheard him, because she steps into the kitchen, hands on her hips. "Leave him alone, Dad. Don't you know Nate well enough to know he wouldn't be involved in anything like that?"

"Just asking a question," he says. I try to say it's all right, that I don't mind a bit, but Mr. McIntyre throws a look at his wife, who's wrist deep in the sink. "You never can tell," he says. It comes out like a loaded statement, and they all pause.

"George," Mrs. McIntyre seethes to her husband. She shakes water from her hands, then wipes them nervously on her thighs.

"Let's just watch the movie," Lorrie says. I look at her, trying to understand what just happened in the kitchen, but she spins away and walks back into the living room, thudding her heels on the floor purposefully.

As we watch the movie everyone stares in silence at the screen, and when I turn to Lorrie to say something she just squeezes my hand tight and nods her head toward the television, refusing to acknowledge anything else.

Chapter 9

We're all stationed in the locker room, sitting in a silence demanded by Coach Harper's top assistant, Spencer Green. Coach is in his office, talking to us one-by-one. He started with the freshmen and sophomores, who might crack right off, while he let the older players stew. He called every single one of us at home last night, requesting our presence in the locker room at seven A.M. Coach didn't say on the phone what the reason was, but everyone knew.

"Son," my father said after the phone call, "you sure you don't know anything about that fraternity?"

"Nothing," I said. I looked up at him, saw the vein by his temple pulsing, an anger I haven't seen in years. It's the look he used to get when Marvin broke curfew, before the transgressions became so much worse that Dad's anger turned to resignation.

"Well, you damn well better be telling the truth."

Coach Green keeps circling the locker room, like he's herding us, trying to make eye contact with players seated obediently at their lockers, but we look down at the floor. Branson, though, is kicked back in his locker with his legs splayed out, like it's a beach chair and he's soaking up sun. He stares right back at Coach Green. "What's shaking, Coach?"

"I think maybe you all know why we're here," Coach Green says.

Green keeps moving, snapping his fingers at Saveen and Luke when he sees them whispering in the corner. "No talking."

Normally the locker room is all bluster and adrenaline, whether it's the stereo blasting pregame rap or Coach screaming after a poor first half or players celebrating after a big win. Even after losses there's some noise, guys kicking their lockers or bitching about bad calls late in the game, the dejected hiss of showers, the thumps of balled-up towels and jerseys into the laundry bucket. But now, with Coach Green enforcing the gag order, all I can hear is the click of his soles, intermittent sighs and yawns, and the nervous scratch of somebody's thumb against his locker. There's the squeak of the door opening, a player returning to the locker room after being questioned by Coach Harper. Then comes the military bark of Coach Harper demanding the next player: "Cole!" It's another freshman, one who wasn't there that day — but there's no telling what he might have learned in the last few weeks.

After what feels like hours, Coach Harper finally walks through the door and calls my name. I start to move toward the door, but it's not fast enough for Harper. "Move your butt, Gilman."

Coach's office is more like a dungeon, dank and poorly lit.

Three of the walls are cinder block painted white, and the fourth is a cage, which separates him from the equipment room, a padlock barring access to the basketballs and wrestling gear and dumbbells. Harper has a barren desk, adorned by only a pad of paper and a pen, and on the pad I can see the roster names printed on each line, freshmen down to seniors, and columns of checks by each name.

"Have a seat, Nate."

Harper huffs once. I can see the lump of the whistle tucked underneath his shirt, like a concealed badge.

"You know what this is about, right?"

"No," I say. I figure it's best to play ignorant.

Harper smacks his hand on his desk and leans across to me, rising out of his seat an inch or two. "Oh, for Pete's sake, Gilman. Don't act stupid." Harper never swears in front of us, always opting for pseudo-expletives, like "Pete's sake" or "that's a bunch of hooey." He starts again: "This is about the robbery at that fraternity. The one where you guys play all summer. The whole dang town is talking about it." He pauses and then adds almost as an afterthought, "They think I got a team of criminals."

"Well, I heard about that, Coach. But we —"

"Shut it." He holds a finger up in warning. "Just answer the questions I ask you. One-word answers — yes or no. You think you can handle that?"

I nod.

"What?"

"Yes."

"That's better."

He turns to his notepad, grinding his jaws. I don't like Coach Harper, never have. He's always tinkering with the offense, trying to incorporate something he saw on ESPN the night before, never letting us just *play*. *Just give us an offense and let us run it*, I've always thought. On top of that, he tries to be a disciplinarian, shouting and acting tough, but I've always thought there's not much behind it, like a dog that does some good barking from the porch. He seems to yell only because he thinks that's what coaches do, or because he's still the youngest coach in the county and he thinks it will make people respect him more. But I realize now, and maybe too late, that he's no fool, and his chin is jutted out with a determination to back up his bravado this time.

"Did you play basketball at the Sigma Chi fraternity this summer?"

"Yes," I say. I figure it's best not to deny things that are completely obvious. If I lie on something that basic, I'm busted for sure. For my answer I get a check on the notepad.

"Did you play basketball at Sigma Chi fraternity between the dates of August 19 and August 25?"

"I . . . well, I'm not sure of every date we played there."

"Yes or no, Gilman. These are the exact same questions I've asked every other player so far, and they haven't had problems answering them. Yes or no."

"Yes."

That earns another check.

"Were there other players from the team present between those dates?"

"Yes."

Check.

"Okay, Nate. An answer that's not yes or no. Who else was there?" He flips the page and I can see a list of names, but I can't make out which ones he has.

I pause, but I know that makes things look bad. "Most of us," I admit. "The guys who play all summer. Me, Saveen, Luke, Branson."

"That's not all."

"No, almost all of us were there."

Coach starts to run down some names, and I answer truthfully each time. Then he comes to Jackson's name, and I pause again.

"Was Jackson there?" he repeats.

"Yes," I say. "He played with us."

"Back to yes or no." Each time he asks a question he looks back up, staring me down, searching for any flinch or tell. "Did you go into the Sigma Chi fraternity at any time?"

"No," I say. It's out before I even think. I say it so fast I almost believe it. There's a check on the notepad, though.

"Did any other players go into the Sigma Chi fraternity?"

"No."

Check.

"Did you take — or even handle for a brief time — anything

at the fraternity, even if it was just laying outside, that didn't belong to you?"

"No."

Check.

"Did any other players handle anything that didn't belong to them?"

"No."

There's one more check on the notepad, and Coach Harper stares at it for a few seconds. Then he looks back to me, eyes cool. "Go wait in the locker room."

I trudge back, feeling a blush rise, and I try not to make eye contact with any of the players who still need to go in. I seek out those who have already been questioned and try reading their silent faces, hoping to tease out what they've said. Have they lied and stayed trustworthy to the team? Or have they been weak and told the truth?

Coach Green walks by and pats me on the head, but I duck away from his hand. He's probably trying to be encouraging, to let me know things will be all right, but I don't want encouragement now.

Finally Coach Harper walks back in on the heels of Branson, the last player questioned. We all look up, expectant. Coach Harper seems bigger somehow, like the knowledge he's gathered has inflated him to twice his normal size, huge with power.

"Everyone back here five minutes after final period," he says. "I would highly recommend getting here on time. Now go to class."

* * *

The key is to keep my head down. In Mr. Davies' class I bury it in my notebook, just writing down everything he says like a model student. In the hallway between classes I stare down at the floor, watch my shadow stretch out in front of me and then disappear each time I move beneath one of the overhead lights. I look at nobody — not my teammates, not the faculty, not even Lorrie as she follows me halfway down the hall issuing urgent whispers: *What's wrong? Why won't you talk to me? What happened?*

By the time I get to lunch I'm convinced the whole school can see through me, and when I see Tuman, the equipment manager Jackson talked to, shuffle past and nod absently in my direction — a guy I've barely thought twice about before now — he seems more like a cop on a stakeout than the junior who picks up our dirty towels.

I pick a seat off in the corner, one of the small, round tables that's usually populated by lowly, anonymous freshmen. It feels safer here, my back covered by two walls, a vantage point on the rest of the cafeteria. I see the team table, the long one by the vending machines we always take. Usually the table is hopping with banter, always a few girls stopping by to socialize or flirt, always checking over their shoulders to make sure Candice or some other girlfriend can't see them flirting, or maybe they're secretly hoping Candice will see, silently wishing for a scene to ensue. But today none of that is happening. The table is sullen, almost motionless, except for them stabbing the food off their trays in a dull rhythm. I see Branson approach them, slap Trey heartily on the back, getting no reaction from the table except for rolling eyes and heads nodding Branson a grudging hello.

I push the food around on my plate, not really hungry, the food in my mouth tasteless, and I find that I'm gripping my fork so tight that it's leaving a groove in my flesh. I scan the rest of the cafeteria, all the social groups compartmentalized off to their own, heads at some of the tables occasionally swiveling toward the team, even though there's nothing happening. By now, I'm sure the whole school harbors the same suspicions. But then again it's always been this way: the rest of the school taking cues from that table. After all, in this town if you're a varsity player you're a social star.

In the hallway, through the cafeteria's tall windows, I can see Coach Harper standing with his arms crossed, biceps bulging, a hand raised to his chin. He's talking with Principal Cash, looks of deep concern on both their faces, and while they never look directly into the cafeteria, they've positioned themselves so they can be seen by the team, a kind of constant reminder that trouble is on the horizon.

I can also see Jackson, who this whole time has been standing at the edge of the salad bar, his plate already full, but unable to leave because people keep stopping to talk to him, people I barely know. They aren't even names, rather the girl with the strange-looking glasses whose father runs the bookstore on the square, the overweight guy — *Garvey, maybe* — who always wears black concert T-shirts, the Goth girl — *an A name,*

Aubrey? Andrea? — who showed up at Saveen's party back in June, uninvited, and then left in unexplained tears after half an hour.

I shove my tray away, check my wallet, even though I know what's there — a twenty and two fives left from what my mom tossed my way last weekend. I decide to sneak out for some food from the convenience store down the street. I walk out, looking back at the cafeteria cut into sections like a map, but with cliques instead of countries. The order of it, the strict social rules of Cheneysburg, makes me almost physically ill, even though I can see that at my table, the one for the basketball team, there's still a spot open where I usually sit.

They banned leaving school for lunch six years ago when a freshman girl was hit by a car while crossing the street, but it's easy to do. All the way in the northeast corner of the school, past the shop rooms and the last bay of freshman lockers, the hallway gets pretty lonely, and it makes a good escape route. Nobody ever sees people scooting out from the door at the end of the hallway, except some of the stoners who are brazen enough to smoke out there, and they're not telling anybody anything.

On the exit, I can always give one last check down the hall. Then, if it's clear, I'm gone, and anyone who happens by will only see the bottom of my shoes getting farther away. But the return approach makes me a little nervous, because my face is exposed to the school and it might be easier to identify me. I've got a strategy worked out where I don't use the sidewalk until the very end, walking along the embankment that leads to the tennis courts and then cresting over the hill only about twenty feet from the entrance. I don't know if it really conceals me, but I've never been caught.

Still, I'm sweating seeing a teacher or Coach Harper or, the way things are going today, even Tuman, who suddenly seems a functional part of the Cheneysburg disciplinary system. Sure enough, I walk in the door and someone's waiting for me.

"Cafeteria food not good enough for you?"

I stop, and it takes a second before my eyes adjust to the shadows of the hallway. It's Lorrie. "Jesus," I say. "You scared the hell out of me."

"Well, you've been jumpy all day. I figured I'd find you coming in here, though."

"Coach Harper called us in this morning." I look around, like there still might be someone lurking to bust me, but the only sound in the hallway is the chunk of wood colliding with wood in one of the shop rooms. "He questioned each of us about the fraternity."

Lorrie's face, which was amused at having startled me, turns serious. "What does he know?"

"That's just it. There's no telling. I didn't say anything he didn't already know."

"Good," she says. Then she looks down and repeats it, as if to herself. "Good."

We start down the hall, which is always dark, like the rest of the school is trying to cloak this wing in shadow and forget it. At the end of the hall, I can see heavy light from the next wing wash the floor in a soft glow, and as we walk I feel a shame come over me, a guilt even deeper than what I felt in the immediate aftermath of the theft. It seems strangely connected to that contrast of light — one wing shadowed and forgotten, the next clear and cared for, the lines that separate everything made distinct.

"Part of me wants to just go tell Coach Harper the truth. Get it all out." I say it almost as a test, trying the words out.

"That's not a good idea," Lorrie says.

"I don't know." I think about my brother, who's called the house more, wanting me to see him again. I want to do that, too, but I'm filled with hesitation, knowing I'll get the same guilt trip from him — at least it feels like a guilt trip, even if that's not what he's trying to do. "Marvin seemed to think coming clean wouldn't be that bad."

"That's not a good idea," she repeats.

We're almost at the end of the hallway, and around the corner I can hear the bustle of the high school. It will be only a minute or two before the bell sounds, until even this hallway will be busy with students making their way to classrooms. "It's the right thing to do, though," I say. "Isn't it?"

"The right thing?" Lorrie says. She pushes me in my shoulder, enough to make me rock back a step. "Nate, the right thing was to not take all that crap in the first place." I start to protest, but she's having none of it, her words picking up velocity as she goes: "But now you've done it, so deal with it. Just suck it up, and wait it out. I mean, think of who you are. You're not some guy like Trey or Branson who lives down on the avenues, who has a father blowing half his paycheck at the liquor store. You're not someone who gets busted for stealing from a shitty fraternity."

"But I *am* one of them," I say. The theft belonged to all of us. But as soon as I say it, it seems wrong. I remember how I felt just before the robbery, when Branson was talking everyone into it, playing off their anger at the rich kids in the fraternity, the ones who come down here every fall from the suburbs of Chicago, driving their SUVs with personalized license plates. But I remember that composite picture of all the frat boys, too — the blue blazers, the almost uniform haircuts, their smiles exuding money — how that could be me one day if I wanted it.

"Oh, really?" Lorrie says. She crosses her arms. "Well, then *be* one of them. But remember, I'm dating Nate Gilman. You. Not Nate's brother, not his teammates who are destined to work construction until they die. You think my parents would let me date any of them? You think I'd want to?"

She storms around the corner then, disappearing into the glare of the light, so abrupt that it's almost white. She doesn't turn to wave this time.

There's not much worse than a wordless locker room, and this is the second time we've been in one today. The only sounds are fingers tapping out rhythm on the benches, throats clearing, gum popping between teeth, a virtual symphony of nerves while we wait for Coach Harper. The assistants are all by the chalkboard, arms crossed, whistles hanging on their chests.

I scan the room and see the players, even Branson, with their heads down, waiting. Even the freshmen who weren't involved stare straight down at their sneakers, like the guilt is contagious and has rubbed off on them. Only Jackson is looking up, straight ahead at the staff, nothing to hide. The door swings open and Harper strides to the front of the locker room, all the other motion in the room ceasing. He holds his clipboard in front of him, the questionnaires he checked earlier today resting on top of it. He stares down at it, then looks at us, then back down to the clipboard. I can hear him breathing loud through his nose. I can hear Luke, next to me, swallow and give the tiniest of whimpers — pure fear.

"Thank you all for cooperating today," Harper starts. He keeps his eyes on the papers in front of him. "We've been able to cross-reference all your answers so we can tell if there's any conflict between what any of you said. We've been able to check for any liars among you." He looks up at us, just for an instant before it's back to his check sheets, almost as if he were reading a speech directly from them. "Understand that nobody — *nobody* — has made any formal accusations about anyone on this team, that everything before today was just rumor. Understand that we had to take these measures, though, because in a town the size of Cheneysburg you can't let rumors run their course, because talk can be damaging. To a person and to a team. So we did this. And know that if you lied today, you will receive more severe punishment than others who didn't, if at any time those lies become evident." He rattles all this off like he's been working on it all day, the clipped tone of a courtroom lawyer building his case to the jury.

He looks at us again, his blue eyes squinting. From my seat near the front of the locker room I can just make out the wrinkles around his eyes, his only sign of age.

"If anyone has anything to add to what they said today, now would be the time to do it."

Nothing. Not even a flinch among us. *Let it come*, I think. *Just let it come, whatever it is.*

"In that case. From what I have from all your answers today, all of you — every single boy in this locker room — played at the Sigma Chi fraternity at some point during this summer, as identified by your teammates. In addition, all of you *admit* to playing there. Good. None of you, however, said you entered the fraternity at any time, and, in fact, none of you say that about anybody else. Finally, each of you says that you at no time borrowed, stole, or handled anything that belonged to the fraternity — aside from using their court, of course." He gives a single, short laugh that comes out quick as a dart. "And, to a man, you all say nobody else took anything, either. There is zero substantiation of the rumors about this team's involvement in the theft from the fraternity."

We begin to look around, wondering if that means what we think it does: *We're off the hook.* Of course, we don't want to look too excited, either. If we're innocent, we shouldn't be surprised.

"You're good boys," Harper says. "Thank you for that. The next time you're in this locker room is in two weeks, for the first practice of the season. After that, we've got four weeks to get ready for the county tourney to start the season. We open on the twentieth with North Workston." He squints a little more, those wrinkles at his eyes gaining depth, and nods his head at us. I can feel my pulse everywhere: temple, neck, wrists. "We'll kick their tails up and down the gym floor," he says.

With that, the coaches perform an almost military about-face and walk in single file into their locker room, and we're free to go.

For the forty feet of hallway between the locker room and the parking lot we have to play it cool. We nod at one another, like we expected this, and a few guys talk about getting ready for North Workston. But once we make it outside, wet leaves like red and brown stickers all over the blacktop, we let loose: high fives, yells of relief, fists pumped into the air. Nobody even has to say what to do next. Never mind the cold — *it is time to ball.* A caravan of cars — Branson's rough-throated and now infamous van, Trey's '87 Nova, barely big enough to hold him, Saveen's older brother's Mustang — snakes toward the park. We peel from four-ways in our excitement, dead leaves and wet gravel spit behind us.

At the court, a switch turns *on.* All that pent-up anxiety spills out completely. The high fives from the parking lot turn into celebratory slaps on the back, and the sighs of relief turn to shouts of excitement and pure bravado. I hear Luke, who ten minutes ago looked ready to cry, telling Saveen, "I looked Harper straight in the eye and told him I was insulted he even asked those questions." Everyone starts claiming they weren't nervous, that they knew it was all going to work out fine.

"What about you, Nate?" Saveen asks. "Were you sweatin' it?"

Jackson bounces the rock to me, eyes me while he waits for my answer. I spin the ball in my hands and line up a deep jumper, still a step off the court. "Shiiiiit," I say, playing cool. "Harper couldn't make an ice cube sweat on the Fourth of July. I trusted all you guys." I let the shot go and bury it to a chorus of *oooohs*.

With that we shoot up teams, and as sure as if someone had called in a technician to fix a piece of machinery, every bit of our timing is back, the game running smooth and quick. Jackson pushes the ball every chance, but it's not just him — everyone seems in sync today, hitting cutters right on time, the post players arriving on the blocks in perfect rhythm, the ball barely touching the blacktop on fast breaks — and with every made bucket, with every back-door and reverse pivot, there's chatter from the other players, encouragement or healthy trash talk. The park is mostly empty now, early October too cold for anyone to enjoy tennis or strolls with their kids, but right now none of us seems bothered by the chill. If people were here, though, they could see the change; they could look up from the softball diamond and know that we're a team with promise, with size and shooters and skill, with court chemistry. They'd see we're a threat for county, for Sectionals, maybe beyond. We're without audience, though. Alone. Only my teammates see me come loose off a down-screen and drop a midrange J or flare to the wing and then drive hard to the hole, floating in a runner I've been practicing. For now, that's enough: the looks of recognition from Jackson, and Saveen calling out cutters as we hustle back on defense.

We only have time to run two games before it starts to get too dark, but the spirit is high at the end. Even Branson seems swept up in it — he works hard on the court without giving in to cheap shots or elbows the way he usually does.

After the games, we talk openly about the season, about our goals and how the schedule plays out, about the other teams in our Sectional who might pose a challenge. I give Jackson a ride home, like old times.

"That's the best run we've had in at least a month," I say.

"You see the spin move Trey dropped on Saveen? That was tight as hell. Mighty. He starts playing like that and we will be tough to beat."

"You're not lying." It's good to hear Jackson talk with such enthusiasm, and for the first time I feel like we're moving past the incident at the fraternity, like the whole thing might be swallowed up by the past.

"I'm sorry I didn't come out there for a while," he says.

"Don't worry about it," I say. I reach over and we bump fists. "It's nothing."

109

I turn onto Spring Street, the storefronts of the strip giving way to modest houses, small and boxlike, some with tidy lawns and attractive porches, others with junk littering the yard and paint peeling away. Jackson lives on the end of Spring, where it Ts into Twelfth, in one of the nicer places.

"It's just that the whole thing really bothered me," Jackson says. "Not just that everyone stole all that shit, but the way you gave in to it so easy. And today, I had to lie to Coach. I mean, I'm not a thief, but I had to lie like one. That might be what gets me the most. You made me have to lie for you." He pauses then, staring absently out the window. "I won't ever do that again."

I pull into his driveway, see the headlights wash against their garage. A porch light pops on, and I see a silhouette at the front window, Jackson's father. "But at least the team stuck together and told Coach Harper we didn't do it," I say. "We had to do it to protect the team, the season."

Jackson sighs. "I suppose," he says. "Though I'm sure a lot of it had to do with not wanting to get in trouble."

We grip hands, clasped at the thumbs, then slide our palms along each other until we snap middle fingers — our ritual parting we haven't done in a while.

"I bet it's what Coach Harper wanted to hear, anyway," I say.

Jackson's climbing out of the car and looks back over his shoulder at me. "I *know* it's what Harper wanted to hear," he says. "I just hope he actually believed it."

Chapter 10

Lorrie's parents aren't talking. Not to me, not to Lorrie, not to each other. In my home it's normal for parents to wander around silently, but Lorrie's parents are usually all talk, asking questions and playing host. Their silence is different from my parents', too — there's something charged beneath it, like there are a million things they want to say, but they are playing it off. With my parents, the silence is simply because they've run out of things to say.

"It's been like that for a week," she tells me. "I don't know who did what, but it's never been this bad before." We're sitting in her room, which isn't too unlike mine: NBA posters, high school basketball schedule taped to the mirror in anticipation. The bed we sit on is the major difference. Hers is made, covered with a pink, flowery bedspread, while back home mine is a tornado of blue sheets and blankets piled on top of the mattress.

"Have you tried asking them?" I say.

"Of course." She looks at me like I said the stupidest thing possible. "But they treat me like I'm five, tell me not to worry about it. My dad said, 'Mommy and Daddy will work it out.' Seriously, he said that. *'Mommy and Daddy.'*"

"Sorry," I say. "Is there anything I can do?"

"Not really. Unless you can make all this go away somehow."

"That would be nice," I say. "I'd like to make a lot of things go away." I lean back on her bed, not sure if I should tell her the next part, deciding after a few seconds to go ahead: "I still can't get rid of the idea that maybe I should just admit I stole the stuff."

Lorrie shakes her head but doesn't say anything, then falls back beside me on the bed. I slide my hand over to hers and we lie back, side by side. Once in a while I turn to her and we kiss for a while, but there's no real passion in it, more like we don't know what else to do. Then we lay our heads back again, staring at the ceiling. I can hear her breathing slow, like she might be drifting to sleep, and I suddenly want to promise her that I'll never leave, as crazy as it would sound to her. She sighs, then squeezes my hand tighter and rolls toward me, nestling her head just below my shoulder, looping her arm across me. I can feel her curves through our clothes, and I trace my finger along her hips.

"Nate," she says. "Do you remember freshman year when there was a big scandal over Mr. Case's history final?"

I'd forgotten, but just the name Mr. Case brings it back. That was the year fifteen people aced the final, bringing claims of widespread cheating, charges that were never pinned on anybody. But for a while about half the freshman class was threatened with marks on their permanent records, as the faculty tried to squeeze the truth out of us.

"I haven't thought about that in a long time," I say. "But yeah, I remember."

"It was Candice," Lorrie says. "She saw a stack of tests on Mr. Case's desk between classes and took a copy. She showed it to me, and I couldn't help myself. I was going to get a B in the class unless I did great on the final, so I took it. I thought it would stop there, but Candice let it get out of hand then. I never thought all that would happen."

It's hard for me to picture Lorrie cheating and lying, and even though I know it should bother me, it seems to make her more human, more vulnerable. She must have been out of her mind with guilt. "Jesus, Lorrie. Why didn't you tell me?"

"I was ashamed," she said.

I stroke her arm, tell her it was so long ago nobody even thinks about it anymore.

"That's just it," she says. "Someday that's how people will think about you guys' stealing from the fraternity. They won't think about it at all, or it will be something that happened so long ago nobody will care."

"I don't know," I say.

"Just don't tell anybody," she says. She squeezes my arm hard. "I can't handle that now. After what you went through with Coach Harper, maybe you're in the clear."

She runs her hand along my chest, both of us silent, and then I ask her what all this has to do with her parents. She

113

doesn't answer right away, starting several times to form a word but then hesitating, but I wait her out, watching her hand rise and fall with my breaths.

"A long time ago," she finally says. "I mean long, like five years ago. I came home and saw my mother and Mr. Gaston on the couch."

Just Gaston's name drags the image into my mind: Marvin walking out of the Hartwells' house, Mr. Gaston with his towel still slung over his shoulder, his white face calling for help. Ray Hartwell putting the basketball down obediently before sprinting toward his house, sobs already catching in his throat. Mr. Gaston reaching out to stop Ray, to protect him from what's inside, removing his hand from Marvin's arm, and Marvin stumbling, barely able to walk on his own.

"They were . . . you know," she says.

"They were having sex?"

"No!" Lorrie says. "No, God, no. But they were kind of messing around. I could tell the way my mom's cheeks were all flushed and Mr. Gaston's hair was all crazy."

"Your mom?" I try to block the image of Mrs. McIntyre and Mr. Gaston making out on a couch.

"I know. I never thought that could happen, either. I mean, she's so straitlaced about everything. I never told anyone."

"You never even asked your mom?"

"No," Lorrie says. She props herself up on her elbow so she's above me, her hair loose so that her bangs hang down, almost touching my face. She blocks out the light coming

114

down from the ceiling, and I can barely make out her eyes, but I can see little tears forming at the corners. I reach up and wipe them away, trying to be tender. "I just wanted nobody to know about any of those things. Ever. Like they never happened. But I feel like I have to tell you now, so you can understand where I'm coming from." She lays her head down on top of my chest, her mouth tickling my neck as she speaks: "I mean, I've known for a long time that people do things that are wrong. But I think they should have the decency not to let everyone else know, too. That's when people get hurt."

"I won't tell," I say. "I won't tell anybody."

She starts kissing all over my neck then, with real passion, sniffing and crying the whole time, her arms pulling us so tight it almost feels like we are sharing the same skin.

I walk in the house to find the phone ringing, the whole place empty. No note on the counter this time, no spending money. My parents have been colder to me over the past few weeks, like they're trying out an experiment, seeing how I'll react and waiting for me to slip up.

I forget the phone, figure voice mail will take it, and plop down on the couch. I flip on the television and find some preseason NBA. It's the worst kind of basketball — games that mean nothing, the stars playing sparingly, and even then they're loafing it. The only interesting thing is the rookies trying to eke out a roster spot. Of course, some of them — the hyped draft picks who jumped straight from high school or after one

115

year at a big-time program — could go 0 for 20 and the coach would still hold a starting spot for them. I don't care about them, though. What I like to watch is the no-names — or, more accurately, the names only real fans know. Some guy who played four years at a small school, some mid-major, maybe got some brief airtime if he took his team to the tournament in March, knocked off a powerhouse. Or maybe a journeyman coming back from an injury so bad everyone wrote him off or guys who were hyped once but have drifted out of the spotlight, their talents never matching their headlines, paying dues a couple years in Europe before trying again to crack the NBA. In the game on TV there are only a handful of these players, but there are hundreds of them all over the world, playing their asses off, scrambling and hustling, putting in those solitary gym hours, spinning the ball to themselves to work on a fadeaway, pressing iron from chest to rack, squeezing everything they've got out of their bodies. And each year, out of these hundreds, maybe a half dozen get roster spots in the league. But out of those there will always — almost always — be one who emerges into a bit of a star in the league, maybe helping his team make a run to the Finals, and the media will all be scrambling to figure out where he came from, doing quirky stories on him. I don't need to see that coverage. I already know it.

The phone interrupts again, but I let it go. I've got my eyes on a kid I recognize from his college days over in Terre Haute, one who everyone thought would be a star but never got much done. I loved watching him when he was in college. An unbelievable athlete, he once dropped a 360 dunk in a game, and I swear he was still rising when he threw it down. The guy could have touched the rim with his chin. But he never had the handles to play at the next level and was undersized, only six-four. It's been a while since he's been out of college, and I have to think this is one of his final chances to make the league. If you haven't made your mark by twenty-five, you're pretty much finished. Nobody wants a rookie that old.

The guy I'm watching gets some quality time, playing for an expansion team that's thin at two-guard. And sure enough, about halfway through the second quarter he slides behind the defense and catches a lob pass, one-handed, and thunders it down. The crowd, which has been damn near sedated from watching guys they don't recognize, goes berserk. High fives in the stands. Kids imitating the dunk in the aisles. "Welcome to the NBA," the announcer says.

Then the phone rings again, insistent. I think about letting it go once more, but then I put it together — the repeating calls again.

"We need to meet," Marvin says when I answer. His voice still makes me hesitate, the way I might during a game when I feel out of rhythm, the pace too fast for me. At the same time, though, I feel a new comfort in talking to him, that very voice on the other end attached to so much of my past. If I look out at the pool, I can almost still see him on the diving board, announcing in that same voice — less gravelly then, but the same voice — his upcoming dive: a flip, a jackknife, a cannonball.

"Sure. I want to see you again." I don't realize it's the truth until I say it, and even then I'm not entirely sure. But everything I fear about Marvin — the danger swirling around him, the memory of the accident, the knowledge he has about the robbery — is outweighed by the simple fact that I miss my brother. I look around the house, all the furniture looking like props on a stage that's been silent and dark since Marvin was part of the scene.

"That's nice. But it won't be fun."

"What's wrong?" I ask. There's something in his voice that's smoldering, an anger that wasn't there the first time he called.

"You know, you told me you'd be around and keep me posted. That was weeks ago."

"Marvin, it's not like that. It's just —"

"Forget it. Be at the park on Saturday morning. Nobody goes there this time of year."

I almost tell him he's wrong, that we played there earlier in the week, but that won't do any good. And besides, he's right: Other than diehards like the guys on the team, nobody in his right mind hangs out at the park once it starts getting cold.

"I can do that," I say.

He hangs up without saying good-bye.

I turn back to the game, and the guy I'm pulling for is still in, but things have turned on him. On the defensive end, he gets backed down into the post, and his man drops an easy turn-around on him, about as easy as if I were guarding Saveen. Then, on the other end, he comes out top to handle the ball some and immediately gets in trouble. It's like the other team can smell his weakness. As soon as he gets it, they're into him tight and he mishandles it, dribbles it off his knee, tracks it down along the sideline, then makes a weak, off-balance pass toward the top of the key. It's stolen, picked clean as a low-hanging apple, and turned into a bucket at the other end. I can see him hang his head, those same old deficiencies in his game haunting him still.

The player's breakdown on the court reminds me of Marvin at times after the accident, how all his confidence was replaced by shame and uncertainty. For the first month afterward, my parents kept him sequestered, either in his room or at our grandparents' place in French Lick. They even took him to psychiatrists, anticipating lasting scars. When he finally started going back out, though, it was never the same. Marvin didn't jump in basketball games anymore, at most feeding me jumpers before everyone else showed up at the park, then staying on the sidelines once the game started, saying he just didn't feel up for it. Out in groups, he no longer was the brash-talking leader of the pack, instead always hanging on the periphery, barely speaking.

He was like that at the county fair — usually an event that had him scheming ways to get free rides or trying to get people to sneak under the fence that separated the fair from the country club golf course, just so security would chase us in vain across the fairways. That summer, instead of prodding people toward mischief, Marvin hung back, content to sullenly eat greasy fair food, his face looking pale in the blinking arcade lights. Without him leading the way, his friends seemed just as sullen, bored with the repetition of a summer in Cheneysburg. Still, I tagged along, happy just to be out with Marvin again, even if he was only half there. That's when a scrawny kid in my grade, Lewis Vardell, came up to our group and did the unthinkable — he slapped Marvin on the back and said, "Hey, shooter," then ran off, trying to escape any type of retaliation. Vardell was a kid who always got picked on, and I'm sure he did it on a dare from some other kids, scared that if he didn't, their cruelty would again be turned on him. But it took our collective breaths, and we just stood there in silence, nobody knowing how to react. I looked toward Marvin, hoping that he would snap out of his stupor and do what would have normally come natural to him: chase down Vardell and exact revenge. Instead, he stared blankly at the ground, then turned and trudged away without saying a word.

At that point I knew I would never have my old brother back — not the one with the spark, the nerve. What was harder, though, was seeing Marvin refuse to rally at all, refuse to even try. While he used to sneak cigarettes in the garage just for whimsy, to see if he could get away with it, in the following months it became a habit, a way for him to smolder in his own fate. Any acts of disobedience went from being mischievous tests of our boundaries to a kind of joyless deviance, as if he felt bad behavior and disapproval were all he deserved out of life.

When our parents confronted him he would come to life to argue, but after the fights died down he just returned to his muted, ghostly presence.

I might have been the last person in town to know about Marvin getting involved with drugs. Looking back, it should have been obvious — his withdrawal from every social scene, his constant lethargy, his quiet resentment toward the world in general — but every time I heard the rumors at school I dismissed them as absurd. Even when Lorrie told me she thought there might be some truth to them, I denied it so vehemently that we had one of our few fights to last more than twenty-four hours. Then, almost exactly a year after the accident, I came home to find Marvin smoking in the garage again, only even I could tell it wasn't a regular cigarette. I stood in the doorway watching him, my bookbag still slung over my shoulder, thinking maybe he'd explain it all — his transformation to this: another Cheneysburg stoner. But he just raised the corner of his mouth slyly, a wisp of smoke seeping out, then finally said, "In or out, man. Don't stand there with the damn door open."

Even after that, even after all the disappointments and hard realities, I chalked it up as a one-time thing, something he was just testing, and I try to hold out doubt, even now, about some of the worst rumors about him. And, even after he dismissed me without a word of explanation, I didn't want Marvin to leave. Though I knew that things would never be back to normal, I refused to *believe* it. Even now, just off the phone with him, if I try hard enough I can believe that the memories of him pre-accident — celebrating a touchdown in backyard football, scamming free ride tickets at the fair — are real, and all those images of him post-accident are forgeries.

It's late when my parents get back. They're still dressed up from a party, but their faces are sober.

"Hi, Nate," my mother says. She puts her hand on top of my head, just patting it.

"Where've you two been?" I say.

"Mayor Chambliss had a dinner," my father says. For him, it's nothing special. In fact, he sounds exhausted by the very statement, put out by the social pressures of knowing the Cheneysburg elite. "What did you have?" he asks.

"Nothing," I say. "Just watched a game, then threw in a movie."

"You didn't eat dinner?" my mother says, like it's an outrage of epic proportions. "Oh, I *knew* we should have left you some money. What can I fix you?"

She throws the light on in the kitchen and starts to work. Cupboards clap open and she starts lining up ingredients, offering a whole array of dinner options for me, apologizing the whole time. Each time she suggests something — spaghetti, a pizza, fish, pork chops — I shrug. I tell her anything is fine with me.

My father watches from across the room, taking off his watch, arranging himself a drink. "Wait, Alice," he says. There's an edge, an authority, to his voice I haven't heard since I was a kid. "Wait. My God, you've been out all night. You don't have to come right home and work."

"I don't mind," she says.

"Well, I do. Jesus, the boy's sixteen years old. If he hasn't learned how to fix one meal for himself without us leaving money or instructions for him, well, Jesus." He turns to me. "You're a little grown to have your mother racing around like this, aren't you?"

"I didn't tell her to start making me anything." I don't even know where his anger comes from. It's not like I've done anything wrong. He must still have his suspicions about the fraternity; there's no other way to explain it, no other reason he'd get this upset over something small when for the last few years I could have lobbed a grenade into our kitchen and he wouldn't have bothered to get up from his chair. He must be afraid I'll turn into Marvin, a mark against his social standing.

He looks at my mother, her eyes dodging back and forth between us. "Stop, Alice. Let the boy do something for himself. Let's go upstairs. Don't worry. He's got two hands. He can open the refrigerator. He can operate the microwave."

He puts his arm around her, and after a hesitation on her part they walk off, his other hand gripping his cocktail. As they go up the stairs, one by one, they look back at me, my mother's face full of worry and apology, my father's barely concealing scorn.

I head to the kitchen and stare inside the refrigerator,

muttering to myself. "I can fix my own dinner. I'm not a *child*."
I want to shout that up the stairs to him, but I'm not used to having to stand up to him. It's like I've been speeding down the interstate at eighty miles per hour and someone suddenly spikes a stop sign in the center of my lane.

Chapter 11

I roll up beside Marvin's car. An early Saturday morning, everyone in town is either sleeping one off or taking the morning easy, not venturing out. It's a nasty day, the first bone chill of the season. Leaves still stick to the pavement and the hood of my car, their edges beginning to curl in the wind. The park is desolate, just my car and Marvin's banged-up sedan, its brown so dull that it looks like a natural extension of the mud splotched all over the park grounds.

Marvin slides across his front seat, rolls down the passenger side window. Our cars are side-by-side, and if someone could see us I imagine it would look shady, two people in their idling cars having a conversation through the windows. Someone watching might expect a wad of cash to appear through one window, a bag of drugs through the other. I can't help wondering if Marvin's made that kind of sale; if the stories about him are even half truth, he's no stranger to such transactions.

"Why don't you just get in," Marvin says. He unlocks his passenger door.

"Where we headed?" I ask.

Marvin shrugs his shoulders: destination anywhere. I feel a snag of hesitation, like there might be some other motive behind Marvin's request. I remember all the rumors, the voices in the hall, the *tsk*s of the faculty at the school after he left: He was on hard drugs, selling them, hooked into some serious trouble over in Terre Haute. "Marvin Gilman's headed straight for the grave or prison," I heard Mr. Case say once, not seeing me in the hall while he talked to a guidance counselor.

"Nate," Marvin says. "It's okay, man. I just want to talk to you for a while."

He starts to pull out, the tires sloshing through puddles. I try to ignore all the misgivings people have about Marvin and relax in the car with my brother, give in to a strange satisfaction of riding shotgun with him. This is how it would have gone with my older brother, I tell myself: Marvin taking me out on rides, letting me hang with his friends, maybe giving me the wheel once we hit the country, let me test my driving skills pre-permit. Marvin as my guide through the years I've already passed: fourteen, fifteen, early sixteen. Tips on dating, secrets to skipping class, how to slide through Mrs. Marsh's tests without studying. Of course, I've figured most of those things out on my own now — maybe riding with Marvin just makes me miss something that never existed.

"I'm gonna be blunt," Marvin says. "You think you can deal with that?"

"Shoot," I say. I tap the dashboard, clipping out a backbeat behind the rhythm of the wipers slapping away mist.

"Honesty is this," Marvin says. He looks at me from the driver's side, squinting. "You're not gonna get away with it."

I don't say anything right away. As much as I like cruising down the open road with my brother, I don't want another lecture — it seems I can't go anywhere without getting one these days. I want to go back to the way it was when we were kids: Marvin cracking jokes about his teachers, coming up with fantastic stories about the neighborhood, inventing small mischief around the house, Marvin's imagination the guide to our days.

"Marvin," I say, "we already have. Coach Harper tried all this and —"

"I'm not talking about Coach Harper," he says. He bangs the heel of his hand on the steering wheel, and it reverberates in a low twang. Ahead of us the road descends in long curves toward the valley — on a good map this road might appear like a thin hair curling wildly toward the Ohio River. As Marvin handles the curves, he resumes talking, his voice low and easy again, as if the bends are lulling him toward calm.

"You can pull anything over on Coach Harper. Hell, when I was a freshman, I remember seeing the whole varsity team at a party that got busted. There they went, the starting five jumping over a chain-link fence in the backyard, beers still in hand. Only Harper never suspended them. Said he couldn't find proof since none of them were arrested. But God, the whole town knew.

"Only we're not talking about sneaking out the back door with a beer, are we? I mean, you guys had a lot more in your hands than a twelve-ounce can. And the police aren't just going to let it go as kids being kids. No way."

His mention of the police jars me. "Have you talked to them? To the police?"

I see his knuckles tense around the wheel, his jaw tighten. "Just let me talk, Nate. Okay? We'll get to that." I tell him fine, go ahead. He explains that the truth always comes out somehow — all the players involved, all the merchandise Branson must still have, the indiscreet way guys will handle the money if Branson ever pays them — and that it would be better for me to control *how* it comes out. Some mistakes, he says, can't be erased or tried over like an equation in Mrs. Marsh's class. "I may not have been the best big brother," he says. "But that much I know for a fact. You can't just pretend what happened didn't."

What he says makes sense. Cheneysburg. Too small for secrets. When we were kids, Marvin and I would dream about growing up and moving to a city — Chicago, Cincinnati, even Indianapolis — where not everyone you met knew your life story. Our father would remind us that there were pleasures in a small town, though, that having people know you can be a tremendous comfort. I wonder if he still believes that.

"I understand," I say. "But it's not easy."

"Never is."

"Just tell me," I say. "Please. Have you talked to the police?"

Marvin sighs. He puts his right hand on top of the wheel and leans over toward his window. He looks old, though I

128

suppose not for his age — it's just that he seems old to me since he's still preserved in my memory as fifteen.

"They've talked to me," he says. "But I held them off for now."

Good news, I think. It will at least buy me some time, figure out a way to convince Marvin that I don't need to own up to it.

"But they can smell it," he adds. "When it gets right down to it I'm not that good a liar."

We don't say much on the drive home, though I remind Marvin of our old fantasies of the city. He surprises me by saying that it might not be that far off for him — if he gets some money saved there's not much keeping him here. I want to argue, say that there are plenty of reasons for him to stay — but aside from my own selfish motives I can't think of any reason Marvin would actually want to stay.

We come up a back road to Cheneysburg, wind past the water tower and a church, the one on the outskirts of town that seems to attract the zealots. Then we pass the small strip mall on University where people are starting to mill about, constantly buying the things to fill up their cars, their houses, their lives. Another Cheneysburg weekend. It's enough to make me want Marvin to turn the car around, bust out of town again, push the speedometer to its limit, and not look back. Instead, he takes a right into the park and returns me to my car. I get out and realize that the day has warmed up a bit and turned the morning rain into a clammy film on everything.

Marvin gives me one more shot before I take off, though.

"Funny thing is," he says, "I think the cops think *I'm* the one behind the whole thing. Bet it's the first time they ever pegged the wrong Gilman brother."

I want to ask the questions: *What have you done, Marvin? Which rumors are true?* But I'm not sure I really want those answers, at least not yet. So instead I stand by my car and watch my brother pull away into the morning haze.

Alone again. No phone ringing, no friends over, no Lorrie, no parents. The silence suits me fine, but I don't know what to do with myself in this giant house. There are times I think I may never get out of this place, like I'm stuck in the heart of a maze. Not that the house is that big, but when it's empty like this it seems hopeless; I understand my mother's desperation at times like this.

I fix myself some lunch and flip on the television, mute another preseason game, happy to see the Pacers are handing the Knicks a drubbing. During time-outs, though, I still get antsy, not content to sit on the couch. I feel like I should be doing something, anything. I try Lorrie, then Jackson, but end up leaving messages at both places. I look at the pool outside, dead and cold. I think back to the summer, hanging with Jackson and talking trash about the upcoming season — all our confidence about taking county, Sectionals, and beyond. Or swimming with Lorrie, stealing kisses or admiring her grace in the water. The daily games with the team over at Sigma Chi, the steady repetition of jump shots finding bottom. All a rhythm I could still understand, keep time to.

Without it, I'm not sure what to do; I don't idle well. But that will all be fixed tomorrow night, with the first official practice of basketball season, a date I've had circled on my calendar since the end of last year, after another Sectional loss to North Workston. No shame in losing to them — they had a senior class that was legendary in the area, with two guys heading off for college ball, one of them even getting Division I looks before he signed with a DII school in Kentucky. We were *pounded*, though, a woodshed beating. Final score: 72–44. And there I was, sitting at the scorer's table, Coach Harper letting me dress varsity for the Sectionals, waiting for a dead ball so I could get some garbage time. I never got in. Half the crowd was already gone, though, so they didn't see me hoping for a stoppage in play that never came, scooping up my warm-ups when the final buzzer sounded and walking back to the locker room with my head down, like a kid who's been sent away from the playground. Like a dog.

But I knew my time would come. We had two shooting guards graduating. Not that they were standouts — that game against North Workston they combined for 3 for 16 shooting. I wanted to scream down the bench at Coach Harper, "I can do better than that." Not like if I got in there and jacked up a brick it was going to ruin the game for us. But that would have gotten me nowhere. I bit my tongue, cut out of the locker room without even a shower, and started getting ready for this season. There might not be a player in the state who spent more time on his game this summer than I did. Open gyms, Sigma Chi, the park, a short summer league over in Terre Haute. Sometimes I'd hit three of those in one day, pushing myself.

Even after hearing Marvin tell me to come clean, I know I can't do it, not with the promises I made to Lorrie, with what I owe Jackson, and most of all with what I owe myself. Not with the hours I put in. Not after how last year ended. No way.

I can hear my dad pull up, the groan of the garage door opening, and I head back to the couch. I jack up the volume on the television, making sure everything looks and sounds natural, as if without the TV's noise my dad might be able to tease my thoughts, my secrets, right out of the air. Normally, I wouldn't think twice about how I act in front of my father, but he still thinks something's up. I've seen the change in him, his eyes more alert and focused than they've been in years. When he jumped me the other night for not fixing my own dinner he seemed like an entirely new person.

He comes in and throws his keys on the table. "Where were you this morning?" he asks.

Straight off, a question. Normally, he'd slip in quietly, silent as a breeze through a window.

"Went over to Trey's house." A safe lie: Trey and I are strictly hoops friends; if I said Jackson's house there's a chance Jackson might have called here during the time I was supposed to be with him. Trey never calls here.

"What the hell were you doing over there?"

"I had to pick up a book for History. I accidentally left it in the class the other day, and he picked it up for me."

"No, I mean, I don't care about that. But you shouldn't be hanging out down on the avenues. Some of those people down there . . ." He trails off, and I see him look down. "Anyway, I don't have anything against the kid, but his parents are not the kind of people I want you to be around. Just have Trey come here from now on."

I stare at him like he couldn't possibly understand what he's talking about.

"Don't give me that look, Nate. Don't think you're fooling me. Just because you play basketball with him doesn't mean you're like him in any other way," he says. Then he adds, "You know that, too."

Maybe he's right: I've been to Trey's house exactly once in all the years I've known him, and then only for about two minutes to pick up a video game he'd borrowed from me. I saw enough in that short time to know I wouldn't be going back any time soon. If our house is sterile in its quiet, Trey's was alive with clamor and menace — his parents shouting obscenities at each other, his younger siblings fighting over the television. There was no physical violence, but everyone seemed at the brink, ready to detonate at any moment, and I thought again about the bruises that sometimes appeared on Trey.

I retreat to the television, pretend like I'm engrossed in the game even though it's only preseason and the Pacers are up twenty. My father plops down in his chair, a tall glass of iced tea in one hand and a bowl of pistachios in his lap. He eats loudly, seeming to take pleasure in the crack of shells. I can't remember the last time we've sat down to watch a game together.

"Basketball," he says. "I tell you, Nate, I just don't see it."

"You don't like hoops?"

"I don't mean that. Sure, I like it. I played some when I was a kid and I always enjoyed playing with you when you were young, but I never thought it would become this big to you."

I shrug. I want to tell him he'd understand it if he'd ever been any good at it, if he ever got that itch under his skin, real as any narcotic. I want to tell him that the feel of a basketball on my fingers is burned into my memory.

"Practice starts tomorrow night, right?" he says.

"Yep," I say. "Midnight on the nose."

He laughs a little. "Like that. What's the point in starting at midnight? Why can't you just wait until after school on Monday and have practice at the regular time?"

He's just trying to get a rise out of me. "You gonna come to some games if I get a starting spot?" I ask.

He doesn't say anything right away; he knows he's been too absent over the last few years. He gets up from his chair, retreating again, not accepting any give-and-take with me. He walks to the kitchen to rinse out his glass, and over the water I can't hear what he says.

"What's that?"

"I said I hope the season goes well."

He heads for the living room, where his bar is waiting, his medication self-prescribed liter by liter to chase down the memory of our family's mistakes. He stops at the entryway, though, turns back to me. His face is obscured, but the buttons on his shirt catch light from the kitchen, standing out almost like stars. "I've asked you before about that story in the paper. I know Coach Harper's asked all of you. I guess, because it's you, I'm inclined to believe you." His head goes down, the bald spot on top showing like a slice of peach. "Your mother and I never expected problems like that with you." His head comes back up, and he clears his throat after stammering on the last sentence. He speaks clearly: "I hope for your sake you're telling the truth."

Chapter 12

Midnight Madness. At colleges all over the country, the same thing is happening: The first practice of the season begins on the stroke of midnight, the very minute teams are allowed to start practicing. At the big hoops schools, of course, there are crowds of thousands, packed gyms, the loudspeakers blaring, coaches giving speeches to rally the students into a frenzy, TV crews broadcasting highlights, freshman phenoms getting their first chance under the lights, seniors back for their last go-round, all of them talking about trips to the Final Four and hoisting a banner for a national championship, the team captain pointing above the scoreboard where the banner will hang when they bring it home months later in ultimate victory. The band starts with a jump, the fight song blasting loud as a jet engine, and the students scream, their faces painted in the school colors, adrenaline fueled by a day of booze and the possibility of getting their exuberance replayed on TV screens across the country. They'll have fan giveaways and local rock bands, and they'll let the players scrimmage, the coach taking the reins off completely, indulging the crowd.

Everyone with a green light on deep threes. Behind-the-back passes. Dunk contests. The works.

In Cheneysburg, though, no crowd. Just us, the coaches, and the gym. No dunk contests, either — a good thing, since it would only be Saveen and Trey unless they lowered the rims for the rest of us. Instead, Coach starts us with the simplest of warm-up drills. "Three-man weave," he says. It doesn't matter. Right now we're so amped the drill could just as well be a fast break to win Sectional Finals. After a long summer and the infighting between us giving way to the solidarity in the wake of Coach's suspicions, after watching the NBA go through the motions in the preseason, after the debacle to end the previous season, seeing Saveen and Trey get better and stronger, watching Jackson fine-tune his timing and add new moves to his game, after sitting outside the gym on the hoods of our cars, waiting in the cold for the clock to turn midnight, after throwing on the practice jerseys, itchy after months on a shelf, after all that, we are as ready as I think a team has ever been.

Every pass pops. The gym is filled with chatter, everyone calling the name of the person they pass to — *Jackson! Saveen! Branson! Luke!* — the squeak of sneakers on the hardwood clear as horns, the shouts of the coaches urging us to push the ball faster, cut harder, the sweet sound of lay-ups finding the net.

Soon we all have healthy sweats worked up as we cruise through the drills: defensive slide, no-travel, loose ball, breakaway, and chase. They're all the drills that test our conditioning, and Harper doesn't let up on any of them, blowing his whistle like a boot camp instructor if he so much as suspects somebody isn't giving his all. Finally, Harper breaks us off for free throws so we can catch our breath, but I see him shoot a look to one of the assistants — eyebrows raised — and I know he's pleased with our intensity and the shape we're in after the off-season. I get the same hoop as Branson and Jackson during free throws, and I can see Branson's chest heaving. His face is flushed, and the scar tissue that runs along the side of his face seems to have turned a bluish purple, like a bruise. I can't help but take some pleasure — that's what a summer of cigarettes and beer and cruising town in your crappy van will do to you, Branson. But I give him an encouraging slap on his shoulder instead. "Keep pushing," I tell him. "You'll be fine."

Branson shoots me a damning glare. "Fuck off, Nate," he says.

So much for sympathy. So much for the team-first attitude. It takes Jackson to explain it to me, though, as Coach calls us to a midcourt huddle. "Don't worry," he whispers. "He's only acting that way because he's scared of you."

Coach splits the team up for position work, post players on one end and perimeter on the other, and we start into shooting drills. Shots off a flare, shots off a curl, shots off a pump and one dribble. Right away I have it rolling in a good rhythm — bucket, bucket, bucket. On my end we have an assistant running the drill, but I hear Harper at midcourt, where he can watch everyone: "Stroke looks good, Nate."

After that we start into the more tedious work, piecing

together offensive and defensive schemes. The entire practice goes well, and even Harper, rarely one to give us too much freedom, is pleased enough to close the practice with the best drill of all, the three-on-two break, basically a constant fast break down one end of the floor and then back the other way with different players rotating in on offense and defense. We invariably disintegrate into showmanship and sloppy play, but I guess Harper figures we've had a good practice and it's almost two in the morning, so what the hell.

Sure enough, we start getting wild. Guys jacking up jumpers from way out of their range or going for lay-ups out of control, double-pumping and flipping up off-balance reverses. I can see Harper getting ready to call it a night, but before he does I get out on a break with Jackson and Saveen. Crossing midcourt, Jackson kicks it to me on the wing, but I hear him clapping his hands to get it back, so I take one dribble to draw the defense, then flip it back to him, and as soon as he touches it he sends it the other way, lobbing it high for Saveen, who's been sprinting the whole time, on a beeline for the rim. The ball floats down right as Saveen rises to catch it, and *boom!*, he thunders it down in one motion, a perfect alley-oop. Sweet glory.

The other players call out their approval, and Harper blows his whistle. "A perfect way to end the night," he says. Harper starts to tell us to shower up and unroll our sleeping bags — the other tradition of Midnight Madness. We sleep at the gymnasium, unrolling our sleeping bags on the mats in the wrestling room, a ritual that is part team bonding and partly so Harper can make sure we all make it to first period the next day. He is midsentence when we see Saveen come up limping. In the excitement over his dunk, none of us saw him hopping around on one foot after landing funny. Immediately the team falls to silence. Harper, clearly unnerved by seeing his best player hurt on the last play of the first practice, swears in front of us for the first time I can ever remember: "Oh, holy shit, no."

Harper catches himself, though, and immediately turns it into a lecture, tells us we never should be trying those kinds of plays. "Always be under control," he shouts. "You start flipping around like that and somebody gets hurt."

"It's all right, Coach," Saveen says. He's still limping, putting a little pressure on his right ankle now. "I just tweaked it. I'll ice it tonight."

That pacifies Harper a little bit. "Fine. But still, lesson learned." He looks at me and Jackson, like we intentionally hurt Saveen. "Always play under control. One slip-up can ruin a practice, a game, a season. Always make good decisions. That's what the game's about." He scans all of us, overly serious, like we should be taking notes or something. "But all in all," he adds, "a good first practice."

With Saveen icing his ankle, I get chosen to help with the food run. Every year, everyone throws in some cash and Coach lets a few players journey out for late-night eats, the run functioning both as an honor and as a test, a way to see if we're mature enough not to do anything stupid when we're cut loose at this hour, and return with precise change.

Trey's in the backseat, a paper towel with a list of orders scrawled on it, and Branson's riding shotgun, holding the money. I'm behind the wheel. Coach picking me, as a junior, is a sign of confidence, especially when there were other seniors available and even an obvious team leader like Jackson.

We don't get two blocks before Branson starts itching for trouble. I can see it in the way he looks at me from the passenger side, a gleam of depravity flickering in the passing streetlights. We're sitting at a red light when he claps his hands, rubs them together as if trying to warm them. "Hang a right here, Nate."

"The place is straight ahead," I say, even though Branson knows that — you'd have to be blindfolded to get lost in Cheneysburg.

"No shit, Mr. Navigator," Branson growls. "My place is down the road to the right."

"We're not going to your place," Trey says, leaning over from the backseat, his head between ours.

Branson shifts in his seat to look at us. "I forgot something there. I just need to swing by and get it."

The light turns, and I cruise straight ahead, ignoring Branson when he starts to yell at me that he really needs to get to his house, to make a turn. I just watch the road, though I can sense Branson looking at me. He leans forward, his head almost on the dashboard, forcing himself into my peripheral vision like a fan at a basketball game trying to get on TV, angling behind the announcers during the pregame show. I refuse to acknowledge him, but Trey can't help himself and asks Branson what he forgot.

Branson leans back and sighs. I sneak a look over at him, instantly angry with myself for giving him attention, and I see him roll his eyes at Trey's question. He laughs. "A little hooch," he says. "I forgot a pint of vodka I wanted to bring." His smile broadens; he's too pleased with his own bad intentions to lie about them.

"No way," I say, and continue driving straight ahead, approaching the restaurant.

"Yeah, fuck that," Trey says. There's anger in his voice, and he pushes Branson on the shoulder, hard enough for Branson to crunch against the side of the car before he swats Trey's hand back. "What do you want to do, get us all booted from the team after the first practice?"

"What? It'll be fun. Coach will never know."

"He'll smell it all over us."

"Vodka doesn't smell."

"Yes, it does. That's just something people always say, but you can smell it."

"Fine, we'll dump it in our drinks from here. Then he won't be able to tell."

"He'll still know."

I listen to them bicker as I pull into the drive-thru, and I have to turn to them and tell them to quiet down, act normal.

For an instant I feel like my father scolding me and Marvin on a long drive on vacation, leveraging himself so hard against the headrest that it seemed ready to snap off.

They shut up long enough for me to read the entire order off, but they're starting to shove each other, the car rocking with their force. Branson raises a fist, ready to swing at Trey in the backseat, but doesn't follow through. His fist just hovers in the darkness like a miniature full moon. Finally he relaxes it as our order is read back to us, distorted through the speaker, and the two stare each other down, each waiting for the other to flinch.

I ease the car up and after a few silent minutes they hand our massive order through the window, bag after bag, and the car is filled with the smell of melted cheese and hot fries. That seems to relax the two, and we're on our way, Branson counting the change to make sure we're straight when we get back.

We get a block and Branson, offhandedly, almost like a joke, tells me again to swing by his house. His tone lets me ignore it, though, and I cruise on back toward the gym.

Branson shakes his head. "What is it with you two? Always have to follow the rules. Boring." He sings out *Boring*, taunting us.

"What is it with you," I say, "that you can't even follow rules for two minutes? You remember where your last little idea got us, don't you?"

Trey barks assent from the backseat, muffled by a mouthful of cheeseburger.

"What?" Branson sneers. "Are we in trouble? No. We got off with the loot, not that those assholes over at the college needed it. They'll just get Mommy and Daddy to buy them new gear, and then all semester they can bitch to their Buffy girlfriends about how horrible it was to be robbed. They'll play it for all it's worth. Shit, it's a fair trade. . . ."

Branson's in full lecture mode, just like he was at the fraternity. I have to give him credit — he can get himself worked into a convincing frenzy. Given different circumstances, he could run for office. Only this time, Trey isn't fooled.

"Hey," he shouts. "Where's our money?"

"Right here," Branson answers. He pulls the wad of cash from his pocket and waves a few bills at Trey. "What, you think I'm gonna make off with everyone's change? I mean, I might be crazy, but I'm not stupid."

"That's not what I mean," Trey says. "You told me a month ago that we'd start seeing the cash in a week or two. I haven't seen a damn dime. What's the story?"

Branson scowls at the question, like he's insulted by it. I realize that it's true: We've never been given any of the money Branson promised us. No windfall whatsoever. I've been so wrapped up in keeping the robbery a secret, I've forgotten that there was actually supposed to be a *benefit* from it. But Trey's right — two months since that day, and there's been no money from Branson.

Apparently Trey's not the only one to notice. "Everyone's asking," he says. "Luke keeps after me about it. He thinks you're stiffing us, that you sold all that crap and you're keeping the money for yourself. But I told him what you told me — that it would take some time to unload it, that you'd need to go to different places to sell it so nobody would get suspicious." Trey slams his hand into Branson's headrest. "That was weeks ago."

Branson starts explaining, but I can hear the defensiveness in his voice. In fact, he just repeats what Trey said, that he can't sell everything right away. "Be patient," he says.

"See," I say. "This is the kind of shit that happens."

"I don't need the lecture, Nate," Branson snaps.

"Nobody needs a lecture," Trey says. He grabs Branson's shoulder, and for the first time I see Branson flat-out flinch, like he thinks he might not be able to take Trey if it comes to blows. "We need the money you owe us."

We're back in the parking lot of the gym now, still in the car. I worry that the coaches might see my headlights and come out, so I shut them off and kill the engine.

Branson wrestles himself from Trey's grip, his back against the door, and stares wildly at us. He grinds his jaw, his chest heaving. "You two," he says. He shoots a finger at me. "You want everyone to be nice, to get along just fine, as long as everyone loves you. Well, it's not that simple." Then the finger swings to Trey, steady as the barrel of a gun. "And you think *I* owe you? Shit, man. We live in the same neighborhood, only I don't get people helping me out."

"What's that mean?" Trey says. He's screaming now, and the two seem destined to have a fight, right here in my car.

"It means I know how you paid for your food tonight," Branson says. "I pay attention. I see things. I saw Coach slide

145

you a five. He did it because your parents didn't give you any fucking money for food."

I think Trey's going to swing at Branson, but he suddenly gives in. His demeanor changes, as if it is ice cracking, falling away to reveal Trey's real face, young and tender. He lowers his eyes, looks at his hands.

"How's that for rules?" Branson says. "It's only five bucks, but it's against the goddamn rules. So don't you lecture me. And don't you push me." He throws the cash at me, sends quarters and nickels tumbling all over my front seat and floorboards. "Here's the goddamn change. The rest of the money I *owe* you will come soon enough. You two just keep your mouths shut and let me handle it."

He gets out and slams the door, the car rocking with his force. I scrounge up the change and then help Trey tote the food inside. Branson has already disappeared behind the thick doors of the gym, and as our shoes scrape across the dirty blacktop I think I hear Trey sniff — either from the cold or in reaction to Branson. We walk into the warmth of the gym, hear the sounds of our teammates rising in excitement at the arrival of the food, most of them still pleased in the afterglow of the first practice. We pass the food out, disperse the change in orderly fashion, acting as if there wasn't a single thing out of place in all the world.

Chapter 13

The second practice — after about four hours of sleep and a full day of classes — is technically on the same day as the first one, and it's always awful. It's almost like a part of the ritual, giving Coach Harper a chance to yell at us and promise that if this is how we're going to play after the midnight practice, then he'll cancel the tradition altogether. So in the wake of it, I'm not too upset. I don't get the worst of Harper's verbal abuse, and we all know it's part of the routine. It's not until Lorrie comes by with the news that I know something is wrong.

"Trey quit the team," she says, the second time she's had to tell me, trying to drive the point home. "Don't look at me like I'm Candice spreading some rumor. I'm not making it up."

She explains that the word is already circulating through town. The women's team practices right after us, and they saw Trey walking out of the locker room, his head hanging down. When they asked what happened, he wouldn't answer, but when Coach Harper walked out with the same severe expression, they knew something was up. "Sure enough," Lorrie says, "I had a message from Emma when I got home, saying that Trey walked."

"Did she say why?"

Lorrie shakes her head. I can tell she's worried about the same thing I am — that Trey came clean about the robbery. Lorrie isn't one to get caught up in gossip for the sake of rumor itself; there has to be some kind of personal investment for her. "But I figure if he talked," she says, "I suppose we'd have heard about that, too."

We're sitting upstairs in my room, and when my mother walks by we stop talking. She looks in but doesn't say anything, just stands there in my doorway as if she's studying herself in the mirror. She tucks a loose strand of hair behind her ear, smiles vaguely.

"What?" I ask.

"Nothing," she says. She does this. She doesn't trust us in my room alone, like five minutes alone up here and Lorrie will come back down the stairs eight months pregnant, our lives ruined. Or maybe she just wants to talk. Either way, she's always wandering past my door when I'm in here with Lorrie.

"Well?" I say.

"Do either of you want any food?" she asks. "There's lasagna left."

We chime a *no thanks* in unison and look down at our hands, nervous under her gaze. Every time my mother does this I wind up feeling like we actually are guilty of something, like she's caught us with our clothes off, our faces flushed, even though that's never happened — things that our parents wouldn't be crazy about, sure, but nothing that would get us disowned. She lingers there for another second, steps in like she's going to adjust something on my dresser, thinks better of it, nods to us, and walks away.

"She's crazy," I say.

"Stop that," Lorrie warns. "You don't know anything about it. You should see my folks."

The last week has brought one change to Lorrie's house: In addition to the moody silences that eat up two- and three-hour chunks, there are also short bursts of shouting, like a volcano releasing pressure, only to return to a simmer. She's told me they don't even fight about anything serious, just things like what movie they're going to watch or who left the orange juice out.

I hear my mother step softly down the stairs to join my dad in front of the television. He has left me alone for the last couple days, and I think that maybe he's satisfied that I wasn't involved in any theft, haven't tarnished the family name any more than his other son already has. Outside, the wind is whipping up, rising in little moans along the road, and I can hear the flag on the front porch snapping. There is a freeze out tonight, the smattering of rain pooling into black ice on the streets, small omens of the winter's menace to come.

"It's horrible at home," Lorrie says. She puts her head against me and sighs. It seems odd, though, like she's trying to act younger than she is, slip back into childhood.

She curls her fingers into my hand, and when I try to lift her face to mine so I can look at her, she shies away, tucking her chin down into her chest. I rub her back, trying to move my hand in soothing circles. I can feel the knuckles of her spine under her shirt, the taut muscles spreading across her back, which rises with each breath, swelling into my open hand.

"It's bad there," she says. "They're not going to put it back together. I can feel it."

I try to imagine her parents the way she describes them. I saw some of it firsthand, their snorts at each other's comments, their narrowed eyes, but it still doesn't compute for me. I've seen her father glad-hand too many people to imagine him not putting the best spin on any circumstance, and I've seen her mother be so sickeningly polite over the years that I can't picture her holding any kind of grudge. Of course, I could never have imagined Mrs. McIntyre fooling around with Mr. Gaston, either, until Lorrie told me about it. But I suppose it's not the first time I haven't known people as well as I thought I did.

"I'm tired," Lorrie says, "of all this."

I'm not sure what to do, so I just keep stroking her back, saying stupid things like *It'll be okay*, things that can't possibly be true. I realize now that Lorrie's always been the one who knows what to do and say and the reversed roles don't suit me well. I feel like an impostor.

"Everything will work out," I say.

"No, it won't," Lorrie says. There's the hint of tears in her voice. "Everything I tried to be — none of it's true."

"This doesn't change who *you* are."

"It changes who people think I am, though. I wanted

150

everything to be perfect. I wanted everyone to think I had every-thing together."

I think back to our night out by Bethel Bridge, near the end of the summer. I remember Lorrie telling me, when I won-dered what people would think about us if we both started on the varsity teams, that it didn't matter what people thought.

"I thought you didn't care about those things," I say.

"I say that," Lorrie tells me. "Sometimes I mean it."

Her admission catches me off guard, like I've spotted a crack running along a foundation I thought was solid. I ask her what she means by *sometimes*.

"I mean that's not always how I feel. Living in Cheneysburg isn't easy for me. There are things people expect out of me — I'm supposed to look good, to be the star player, to make straight As. Don't get me wrong — I want to do those things. It's just there are times I feel like I'm chasing a goal other people set for me."

"We all feel that way," I say, trying again to soothe her. "Just because you feel that kind of pressure doesn't make you wrong."

"Fine, but if people expect things out of me, you better *believe* I expect something in return." She pauses, taking a few breaths to calm herself down. She nestles into me a little closer, as if trying to soften what she's saying, though her voice is as determined as ever. "I mean it. It's like I've made a deal with people, and if I live up to my end of the bargain, they should, too. That goes for my parents, and for you."

I know exactly what she's getting at: I'm to keep my mouth shut and appearances up, the same thing she warned me about when I suggested to her that I should admit the theft. That is a facet of Lorrie I'm learning about quickly, but it raises another question, one that's been bothering me since we visited Marvin.

"If you care about what people think — about the standards you're supposed to keep up — then why did you date me after Marvin's accident? Why do I still meet those standards with my brother being who he is?"

When I ask the question, I think it will make her pause, maybe even re-evaluate the standards themselves. She doesn't miss a beat, though. She pops up on the bed and looks directly at me, answering while she pulls some loose threads of hair back from her face, tidying them.

"Because you handled it so well," she says. It shocks me, because that's the last way I would describe how I handled it. "I'd already spent enough time here to know how much you loved Marvin, how much that had to hurt you. But you never talked about it to anyone, like it didn't happen. Even when he got kicked out of school, you didn't change around other people. I knew you were hurting on the inside, but from the outside it looked like all that was happening to some other family altogether."

After Lorrie leaves, I try calling Trey but only get a busy signal — a near impossibility these days, but his family has never bothered with call-waiting or voice mail. I can only assume that the phone is off the hook, Trey getting the worst of his father, who I'm sure didn't take the news of his son quitting the varsity basketball team well. I call Jackson and he agrees to swing by, though he doesn't sound enthusiastic. The rest of the night I spend dodging my parents and wondering about all the forces at play in Cheneysburg — weighing Marvin and the truth against Lorrie, the team, and our cover-up. I try to imagine the town again, the way I could in the summer, without the complications it brings. I think of Lorrie and me together, our friends grown and still part of our lives — as if I could launch us off into the future, land us in a time so far from now that all this is forgotten, in a place where we are freed from the past.

But it won't ever be that simple. I have been in Cheneysburg long enough to know that stories never end that way. I've seen older brothers go off to college only to come trudging back a year later with only longer hair and deeper debt to show for it, seen high school sweethearts marry, have children, and divorce all within two years of getting their diploma, and I've seen friends turned into enemies, done in by the long days in the mills, the long nights in the bars, and all the small betrayals that stack up in between.

I walk out in the cold and shoot on our driveway hoop, the arc of my shots playing out in shadow beneath the house lights. I hardly ever play out here anymore — the goal is actually about six inches short, and the driveway isn't big enough to really practice. The hoop was only something for Marvin and me to use as kids. I can see my breath come out in puffs in the cold air, hear the ball's bounces echo off our neighbor's house. I keep shooting, though, hoping the repetition will smooth out my thoughts, tamp down my anxieties.

When Jackson arrives, he shoots a couple and then we go inside. He's quiet tonight and doesn't seem bothered by Trey's quitting. He doesn't say much when I ask him about it, wondering out loud if Trey quit because of guilt, because of Branson, because of his father. Or if he'll finally talk about the robbery.

"The guy's got to do what he has to do," Jackson says. He's in his distant mode, pulled back inside himself and unreachable. He's kicked back in my dad's chair in the living room, reclining in complete ease.

"What about the team?" I ask. "We need Trey at forward big-time."

"I'm aware of that," Jackson says. "I don't know if we'll be able to replace him." Only Jackson doesn't look concerned. He reaches down beside the recliner and plucks a magazine from the end table, starts flipping through it. His face droops into a look of study, like he's enthralled with my dad's five-month-old edition of *Forbes*.

I walk over and snatch the magazine from his hands, angry with his indifference. He doesn't even look up at me, just reaches down and grabs another magazine, resumes flipping. I grab that one, too, only he clamps his hand down this time, tries to rip it back toward his chest. We play tug-of-war for a second;

then I decide it's ridiculous to be fighting like this and let Jackson have the magazine. He smiles at me, finally looking me in the eye.

"You give in too easy," he says.

"What the hell is that supposed to mean?"

"I mean, I knew you'd give up on that. Stupid as it is. Just a goddamn magazine." He tosses it over the arm of the chair and it flutters down to the floor, crashing in a flailing of pages, like a bird that's been shot down. "But you're the one who gave in. You always are."

Jackson starts to list ways I give in too easy: any time Lorrie calls me at the last minute even if I have plans with the guys; any time Branson gets overly physical on the basketball floor; the end of last season when I sat by the scorer's table as the game wound down, then didn't utter a word to Harper about how humiliating it was; the way that I answer questions in class like I'm issuing an apology. "Even when you know you're right," Jackson says, "you're still scared to death you're going to be wrong. You wind up looking at me or Lorrie or Saveen for approval."

It's like having somebody play back a game film filled with just my turnovers and the times my man scored on me. I feel a stab with each accusation. But just like watching a film, there's no denying any of it. Every word Jackson says is true and I know it.

I don't let him play his final card, knowing where he's leading. "And that day at Sigma Chi," I say. "I gave in then, too."

"Damn straight you gave in." Then he looks away again. "Took Branson's side over mine."

"That's what this is about?"

"Damn, Nate. You were supposed to be my friend."

I step back from him as if his words were a slap. I sit down on the footstool in front of my mother's chair. I put my head down into my hands. "I'm sorry" is the only thing I can find to say.

There are some creaks on the stairs, and we both stop. The hall light flicks on and I hear my father's voice waver: "Is everything all right down there, Nate?"

"Yes."

"I thought I heard yelling." Just that, the slight tinge of accusation, his unwillingness to completely accept my one-word reply, is a sign of his increased suspicion of me. Normally, he'd just pad back up the stairs. Normally, he might not have checked on us at all.

"It was just the television," I call out. "I'll turn it down."

There are a few seconds of silence. I can almost feel him considering another question, but the light flicks back off and I hear his steps recede.

When I turn back to Jackson he's pointing upstairs to where my parents' room is. "That's another thing," he says.

"My father?" I say. "Jesus, Jackson. I walk all over him. It's just that he's been on my ass more in the last three weeks than he has been in the last five years."

Jackson looks down at me with a disappointed expression. The consideration of his words is evident on his face. Finally he talks again, his words coming out steady. "Why do you never come to my house, except to pick me up?" he asks. "Why is it that I always have to come over here if we're going to hang out?"

"I come over to your house, Jackson. I —"

"Stop it. When's the last time you came over for more than five minutes?"

I can't answer. Again he's right, and I see his point. Just like my father's lecture about not going to Trey's, he gave me similar instructions about Jackson's house long ago — it's okay to be friends, my dad seemed to say, but there were certain lines I should respect.

"I'm not saying it's you," Jackson continues. "I know enough about your dad to know how he feels about the rest of this town. But what's amazing is that you think I don't notice. You think I don't see that? You think guys like Trey and Luke don't notice it, too?"

Jackson puts his hand on my shoulder, a warm gesture to let me know he's not angry, but it turns out to be the worst thing of all, because what I feel in his hand, and what I hear in the tone of his voice, is simple pity for me. *It's not your fault you don't get it*, he seems to be saying.

"Even on the floor, man. You're the one always calling for the ball. And I'm not saying you can't shoot. Hell, I know you can — that's why I kick it to you. But it's like you think the whole team is geared to set you up, like every possession we should concentrate on setting screens for you."

"At least I'm not giving in then," I say, almost hoping it.

"Well, you do if a few shots rattle out. I don't know, Nate. Maybe I'm just talking shit. And I don't mean that I hate you for it or anything, or that we're not friends. We are. Things will be cool. It's just that the whole thing this summer kind of brought it to a head. And once you finally got over that, then Trey quits and you end up seeing that only in terms of you. It's always about you. You ever think Trey quit because it was *his* decision?"

Jackson walks back across the room again, sits down. He puts his head down, looking tired and defeated, almost as weary as my father after a night's worth of cocktails. He looks over at me, his eyelids drooping, and even after all he's said he doesn't seem to take a satisfaction in telling me off; instead, he seems overwhelmed by it.

"What do you want me to do, Jackson? Do you want me to quit the team, too?"

He shakes his head. "No, Nate. We got enough problems without Trey. You just have to make up your own mind for once. If you feel guilty about this summer, then do whatever you have to. Just quit trying to drag me into it, or make me say that it's all okay."

Jackson walks over to the TV, flips through some DVDs. "Either way, let's just move forward, okay?"

"You got it, Jackson."

"Mighty," he says, but I don't believe him. "Now let's watch a movie."

Later, when I drop Jackson off, I see the porch light is still on, a silhouette visible through the drapes in the front window. I look down at the car's clock: one thirty A.M.

"Damn," Jackson says. "They're gonna bitch at me for being out this late."

"Well, next time I'll watch a flick at your house, and I'll be the one that gets yelled at for coming in late on a school night."

Jackson bumps fists with me and nods. He's off, and as Jackson's feet hit his porch I see the silhouette rise inside, moving to greet him at the door. There's no big confrontation, though, just a stern look from his father, who also looks out to my car, squinting in my headlights and nodding in my direction. I've met Jackson's father several times, and I know what will take place inside will be nothing like what happens in Trey's house. There will be no screaming, no violence, just a soft-spoken lecture, probably stressing responsibility, the expectations Jackson's parents have of him.

I drive away and think about Jackson's family and the reasons why I don't spend more time there. I consider the accusations Jackson made, how my father disparages every other part of town: the campus slums where Marvin lives; the small, tidy row houses in Jackson's neighborhood; the sparse country housing on the outskirts of town, barren and cold in the winter; and especially the houses on the avenues, the haunts

Trey and Branson know, the alleys filled with dogs sniffing around garbage and broken glass. Each of these areas, no matter how different, no matter who lives behind the doors, is met with similar disapproval from my father, like nothing else is good enough, like respect in Cheneysburg ends at our neighborhood's property line or, better yet, at our own front door.

If he only knew.

Chapter 14

Two weeks down, two weeks to go. That's how much time we've had to practice, and how much time we have until we open with the county tourney, the big game with North Workston on the first night. Each year the four county schools play a two-day tournament, which not only settles early-season bragging rights but also sets the tone for the rest of the schedule. Coach Harper has the date written on the locker-room chalkboard, and each day reminds us how many days are left until the tourney, erasing the number he wrote the day before. Practices have gone well for me, and I'm getting more time with the starters than Branson, a promising sign. Jackson and I have found our old court rhythm, enough to coax a few compliments even from Coach Harper, who's not one to give empty praise. What has him most impressed is my newfound interest in setting up my teammates — post feeds to Saveen, crisp skip passes for Luke, cross-screens for Jackson, even the occasional drive and dish.

"It's an ever-loving miracle," Harper declared once. "Nate Gilman's discovered the bounce pass!"

That comment drew a few laughs, but I can tell my teammates

appreciate the work I'm doing for them, and I realize now just how selfish a player I was before Jackson called me out on it. Of course, it's not without personal benefit to me — not only have I seen increased time with the first team, my teammates also seem more willing to get me some touches. It seems like every screen I set is repaid to me twofold, and every time I hit somebody for a shot he's looking for me the next time down.

The loss of Trey has been felt, though. Saveen has little help on the boards, and we don't have that second scoring punch down low. At times we'll have to play Saveen with four guys barely six feet tall. It will look like an uncle playing with his four little nephews, and it doesn't bode well against North Workston, who start three guys over six-four. We have a freshman, Freddie Chewes, who is already six-seven, but he's a project, entirely uncoordinated, not used to his height yet, and so skinny he wouldn't leave tracks in fresh snow. We'll have to play him some, but he's at least a year away from being effective.

There are rumors — Cheneysburg churns them out like products on an assembly line — that Trey will come back, that he's expressed second thoughts and will beg Harper's forgiveness. But when I asked Trey, he said he was out for good. "I miss it," he said, "but I can't take that shit anymore. Dealing with Branson, lying to Coach. Besides, I got other stuff to worry about." He's taken a waitstaff job at a local restaurant, earning a wage during hours that would have been filled by basketball practice. The other day he showed up at school with a deep gash on his hand that ran up the back of his wrist until it was concealed under his shirt, like a river cut off by a map's edge. I was about to ask, but he tugged his shirt down tighter over his wrist and balled his hand into a fist, the skin around the cut crinkling so fresh blood seeped from under the scab.

For Harper's part, he's never mentioned Trey except to confirm that he quit. Harper is pointed straight ahead toward the county tourney, like a dog on a scent. I don't think he'd take Trey back anyway.

But despite those changes, we all have our rhythm. Class, practice, homework, a movie at Lorrie's, kissing her lips and neck between low talks about her parents' running feud. Or class, practice, ditch homework to play video games with Jackson — a couple of times at his place. And now, midway between our first practice and our first game, that rhythm changes. I walk out of the gym, postpractice, my hair still wet from the shower so a few brilliantly cold drops get pushed across my forehead from the November wind, and I see him: Marvin, the brother I can't stop thinking about, the brother whose presence I've still been ignoring. I wouldn't think that others would recognize him, but he's drawn the attention of the players who've already made it out of the gym.

Luke sidles next to me. "Nate, is that your . . . your, you know?"

"My brother," I say, finishing his thought for him. "Yeah, it's Marvin."

Luke mumbles something and slaps me on the back.

I see Branson across the parking lot, eyeing the situation.

163

When he sees me looking at him, he cocks his thumb and finger into a gun, twitches his index finger like a trigger. It is so cruel, I can't even think to react, just stand there dumb in the wind-whipped parking lot. Luke, full circle from the summer, is now the first to my defense — or, really, my brother's. "That shit is not funny, Branson," he yells. "You think it's a fucking joke?" He walks toward Branson and the two stand across from each other, each of their chests swelling, and though I know Branson could snap Luke in two without breaking a sweat, he backs down, rolling his eyes and laughing off the situation. I look back and see most of the team gathered by the gymnasium doors, huddled and watching.

I walk straight to Marvin's car and climb in, not caring what they think. I reach over to bump fists with him, but he extends his hand with the palm open, for a standard handshake. I open my hand and he grips it tight, my knuckles rolled in his grip — a man's greeting, I suppose.

"Nate," he says.

"We going for another drive?"

"Just across town."

This time, Marvin gets to it right away. The cops have been watching him, he says, and immediately I get the old visions: syringes in his bathroom, drug money stuffed in his drawers, Marvin's drugged body slouched on his futon, medics trying to revive him. All those rumors that swirled around my brother, the stories of his addictions and exploits spoken in cut-short whispers when I come near.

He puts the car into gear, and we roll out of the parking lot. Outside my window I can see the whole team staring in awe at our exit, and over by the gymnasium, silhouetted in the light behind him, Coach Harper stands in the doorway with his arms crossed in inspection of the scene.

"I just wanted to talk to you again before I leave," he says.

"Leave?"

"In a couple weeks. There's some stuff I want to give you, though."

I want to tell him that leaving won't solve anything, that he needs help, that I can help. Instead, I blurt out, "Don't go."

"Like I said, not much left for me here," he says.

He offers no other explanation, as if he didn't even hear me. Or if he did, my plea didn't even count. Watching him drive, so nonchalant after making his announcement, makes me feel like I'm standing at the edge of his room all over again, watching him pack his things. But as hard as it was to see Marvin leave, I had begun preparing myself for it — after seeing him smoking pot in the garage, it seemed inevitable that the precarious balance our family had wouldn't last much longer. This declaration of departure, though, I had no time to consider beforehand. It's not that it hurts in the same way as the last time — over the past few years I've grown used to thinking of Marvin as "gone." But there is a difference between thinking of him that way, and having his absence be real, Marvin living not just across town, but beyond it, sprung free from the Cheneysburg limits. I try to think about how my parents will react to Marvin leaving town, starting a new life elsewhere, but it's hard to picture, hard to tell if they'll even *know*. Unless I report back, who else would speak a word to them about Marvin?

We roll through town, Marvin's headlights smearing across the dark storefronts, the town quiet and sleepy even though it's only six o'clock. There are signs, though, of everyday life unfolding, the rest of the world oblivious to Marvin's decision. Minivans idle in drive-thrus as the attendant hands over sack after sack of food, and in the liquor store parking lot puffs of exhaust plume when men start their cars, a hefty sack of booze riding shotgun in each. It all gives the evening a lazy feel, but every time headlights swing into view behind us, I think it's the police, ready to clamp down on Marvin once and for all.

When we get to his apartment and walk across the parking lot, I get the urge to yank my collar up to hide my face — Sigma Chis are drinking on their back porch, their cigarettes flaring orange in the night, and I feel like they can sense the guilt on me, like it's all been a setup leading to this moment. But they say nothing, as if they are entirely unaware of our existence.

Marvin's apartment is clean, some of his belongings already packed into boxes. I suppose I expected absolute disarray, the chaos of a man on the run, but even the apartment's foulness that I noticed last time — the lurking sour smell, the papers piled in the corner — has vanished. If anything, Marvin seems to have grown more orderly in the past month.

"Where are you going?"

"Chicago, I guess. I got a friend I can crash with there until I find a job." He jerks his thumb toward the boxes. "Most of those will go in storage for a while."

"What are you gonna do there?"

"I'll find something," he says. His eyes narrow; he's annoyed with my questions. "At least I won't be in Cheneysburg anymore." He shakes his head at the very notion of the town, the pressures it's put on him over the years, and I know that even if he's become an adult, his biggest motivation for leaving is still that same itch he had growing up: out, out, out, the desperation to yank free from the shackles of a small town.

Marvin squats on the floor and starts to dig through one of the boxes, setting down its contents in order on the floor — books, a camera, a pair of dress shoes with a gash in the leather. He looks deeper into the box, mutters to himself.

"What are they after you for?" I say.

"The police?" He looks at me, his head cocked slightly as if he's looking at something crooked on the wall. A smile spreads across his face, and he rubs his chin, his fingers scratching over the stubble. "What do you think?"

I start to answer, but then catch myself short. I see the game. Whatever I say, my answer automatically becomes something I suspect of him, too. It's not an answer but an accusation.

He saves me the trouble, though. "Damn, Nate. I told you the other day that the cops think I'm one of the guys who boosted all the stuff from the frat. They're after me for that."

I'm ashamed for imagining other crimes, for surrendering to the cruelest of Cheneysburg's rumors, but at the same time I'm shocked that the police would have the audacity to point errant fingers at my brother. "But you didn't do it!" I shout.

"I know," Marvin says. He folds up the one box and moves to the next. "You did."

I shut up then, seeing the corner I'm in. I walk over to the futon, take a seat. I take inventory of the place again and I realize that it might not be my parents' house, but Marvin has carved out a life for himself here, that he's become an actual adult on his own.

"I did some things," Marvin said. "But not that. I didn't do half the things people think."

"Like what?" I ask. I can't help myself now. I need to know.

"I know the rumors, Nate. Yeah, after the whole thing when we were kids, I got into some trouble. I messed around with some drugs, but I was never a dealer. And I still party now and then, around town. But it's nothing big. You'd think I was a goddamn high roller if you listened to people, but I've got a life, you know. I had to quit worrying about those things."

"I'm sorry," I say, but it's almost as if he doesn't hear me.

"I did do this, though," Marvin says. He finds what he was looking for and tosses it to me. It's a picture of the two of us with the Hartwell boys, Ray and Jeff, the summer of the accident. We were in the Hartwells' driveway after one of our games of two-on-two, the ball still in Jeff's hands, the goal standing like a monument behind us. Our faces are all smeared with dirt and sweat, our hair blown into wild strands, except for Marvin's, which was always shorn close then. If it were four other boys it would be a picture of innocent youth, a relic of simpler times, but for me there is no nostalgia, no mysticism. There's just the four of us, plain as day, no denying or escaping it — those are the people we used to be. And not long after that, everything was changed. Jeff dead, Marvin in short-lived therapy sessions, Ray packaged off to another school by his parents, reappearing years later with his hair down to his shoulders, his eyebrows home to rows of silver studs, the smell of marijuana wafting off his coat. And there's me — Nate Gilman, who's become who-ever it is that I am today.

"Where'd you get this?" I ask.

"Jeff's mom gave me an extra print when she had it devel-oped. Before, you know." Marvin looks down, picks at his own fingers. "You remember the day in the picture?"

"There were a million like it."

"Nope. I remember that day perfectly. Mrs. Hartwell took that picture and then she made Ray go with her to the store to get new shoes, left the three of us alone. You remember what we did?"

I shake my head. Marvin just stares at me, his eyes hard and cold as drills. Without saying a word, I've lied to my brother again, and he knows it. I remember what happened that day.

"We've never really talked about it," Marvin says. "Not about any of it. You remember that day, don't you?"

I nod my head yes this time. That was the first day Jeff

showed us his father's gun. He handed it to us gently, holding it up on his fingers like it was a cat that might jump. We all took our turns with it, and I remember the cold weight of the gun, being surprised at how heavy it was, how I almost dropped it the first time before grabbing onto the butt, the dimpled handle hard and rough in my fingers. We were amazed by it, and for a while we spoke in whispers even though nobody else was in the house, like any sudden noise might break the spell the gun had on us. After a while, though, our volume increased, as our gentle handlings of the gun turned into practice draws and poses, pretending to pick birds off branches or drop the flag off a mailbox a block and a half away. Then Mrs. Hartwell's car rolled back up the driveway and we packed the gun back into the drawer, folding Mr. Hartwell's socks and underwear back on top of it, moving with quick precision to cover any trace. It was a routine the three of us would get to know before it went awry — that sound echoing down off the driveway's pavement and through the neighborhood. Mr. Gaston walking across the street with the towel over his shoulder, Ray anxiously licking the corners of his lips, Marvin's shirt covered in blood.

I acknowledge it now, admit to Marvin that I remember handling the gun, that I remember all of it. We talk in stops and starts, trying out the words as hesitantly as we first held the gun, then getting to the heart of the matter, diving into the deep places we've never gone before.

"I remember Jeff was drawn to it like some kind of drug," Marvin says. "And each time he kept talking more about

170

actually firing it, like just looking at it wasn't enough anymore. But we never did. He'd cock the thing and aim at nothing in particular, maybe into his parents' closet. I remember putting my hands over my ears, thinking he was actually going to fire, but he never did."

"I don't remember any of that," I say.

"That's because you weren't up there. Jeff wanted to go up there without you sometimes, like there was more risk with less people. I'm sure he took the gun by himself sometimes, too. But that last time — Jesus, Nate, we weren't even being careless. I remember getting scared when Jeff would mess around, trying to spin it on his finger and almost dropping the thing. But it wasn't like that at all."

Marvin squats on his haunches and taps out a slow beat on his knee. He won't look at me now, but there's no fear in his eyes — just a distant stare, as if he can actually see into that place in the past, the one he's never spoken about, as far as I know. Not to me, not to the police or parents or frustrated therapists. But now it comes.

"Nate, I was just putting the damn thing back in the drawer. We were going to come down and play two-on-two with you and Ray. And I thought I had it all the way in there. Put away, you know. But the drawer was still open and my hand, it just kind of got caught on one of the socks, like it got wedged between my hand and the gun." He takes a deep breath now, one last gasp before diving in all the way. "Stupid. Jesus, my hand just got tangled in there. A stupid fucking sock. And so I kind of try to shake it loose. That's all. Not even thinking about it, but my finger is still hooked on that trigger. It's like for a moment I just forget about it altogether, and kind of jerk my hand back and yank it out, but my finger's still hooked on there, like the gun's grabbing me instead of vice versa. Jesus, Nate. Jesus, it's so loud when it goes off, the first thing I think is that we'll go deaf.

"It wasn't like in the movies, though, where there's just this one drop of blood and then everyone slowly realizes what happened. No. I look for Jeff, but he isn't there, isn't standing there. He's down on the floor already, holding his chest, looking up at me. When I bend down and try to pick him up, his eyes are all squinting, in pain. He looks like he just caught me in a lie. Like I've punched him or something. Like he thinks I meant to do it."

"You didn't mean to, though," I say, half statement and half question. Marvin doesn't respond right away, staring down at his hands instead. His eyes look unfocused, though, the same vacant glaze I sometimes see in my parents when they're watching television after a few drinks, the look of people drawn deep inside themselves, insulated in thick layers of memory.

"No, I didn't," he finally says. He eases off his haunches and sits back against the wall, his back making a solid thud against it as he looks up at me. "But it happened anyway. And I was old enough to know what could happen going up there with that thing, handling a gun. I didn't mean to, but it was still my fault."

I almost leap forward from the futon, arguing. "Marvin, it wasn't. It could have been any of us. We were all up there. It could just as easily have been me."

And there it is. It could have been me pulling that trigger, kneeling over another boy, and getting blood on my shirt, marked as trouble all my future days in Cheneysburg. One brother pegged as a felon, the other with his future wide open — it could have been the other way. I've always known it, I suppose, carried it around as a part of me, like a tattoo or a scar, something so much a part of my skin I can almost forget about it, but this is the first I've ever admitted it to anyone, and speaking those words makes it seem more real, like some kind of fossil has been unearthed for us to inspect from all angles. If it could have been me, then why do I get treated better than Marvin? If he could have just as easily been the good brother, then why is he treated like an outcast? Would he be the one the cops were after for the fraternity? Is it just blind luck that makes everyone think that Marvin is twice guilty, that I'm the good son, the innocent on the honor roll?

"It wasn't you, though," Marvin says. "It was me. It took me a long time to get over that, and in some ways I never will. But I'll tell you what I *am* over. I'm over thinking I'm the one who was hurt that day. For a long time, I was angry, because I knew it could have been the other way around. Hell, Nate, I was angry at you. And I wasted a lot of time being angry at you, at myself, at Mom and Dad, at the whole town. But eventually I had to just deal with what happened, and realize that I couldn't go back and change it. Nothing can be changed once it happens. You just have to do the best you can with the history you make for yourself."

Marvin comes and sits next to me, puts a hand on my shoulder. We sit there in silence, hearing an occasional blast of music from next door, or the rev of a car's engine. When Marvin's heater kicks in it sends a small vibration through the floorboards, just enough to make the picture of us as kids tremble on the table. My older brother presses his hands on my shoulders, telling me that everything's going to be okay. In his own way he is telling me the truth. And, in a way that I think I understand, he is telling me a lie.

Chapter 15

Nobody is making me do this. There's pressure to, sure. But there's been just as much pressure not to. I do it early in the day, before I can see Lorrie and change my mind. It's been a week since my last visit with Marvin, and Lorrie's been at me, asking me why I'm so quiet, what's going on in that head of mine. But there will be time to try to make things right with her later — I can't worry about it now.

If I were to answer her, though, I would tell her that my conversation with Marvin keeps replaying in my head, along with the old images from the Hartwells' house: Jeff handing the gun to Marvin, then Marvin handing it to me. What happened to Marvin — what happened to *Jeff* — could have happened to any of us. And if chance gave me a free pass then, I have to accept the blame for more recent actions. In reality, though, it's not only my feelings of guilt for Marvin. There's Jackson, too. He was right when he said that I turned him into a liar simply because I was unwilling to stand up, just once, to Branson. Over the past week, during the routine of practice, during the silent dinners at home, and during those sleepless hours after

175

the lights go out — nothing keeping me awake but the noise of my own conscience — I keep seeing Jackson's look of betrayal, and I start to wonder if an act of solidarity to most of the team really outweighs an act of disloyalty to a friend.

Of course, in the end, it's more than either of those things. I know that I have made my friend and my brother play false roles, made them pay for crimes they did not commit, but it comes down to the fact that I am a phony. I cannot escape that, no matter how much I wish I could. Lorrie would argue that it is best to keep up an image, but she's wrong. It just doesn't work. Not for her, not for people like my father, and not for me. In the end, image is nothing if it's built on a lie.

So I come to Coach Harper's office this morning trying to keep that idea in mind. He looks up from his notepad, taps the eraser of his pencil on his chin. "What brings you here this early, Nate?"

I don't say anything at first, just pull up a chair, its metal legs scraping across the floor. The office looks the same as before, only Coach Harper's look has changed. Instead of trying to look tough, ready to give me an interrogation, he looks pleased, almost expectant. There's no list of names on his paper now, rather some rough diagrams of offensive sets, his latest strategic breakthroughs. He offers me a sympathetic smile, and I imagine he thinks I've come to chat with him about a problem, something personal — in between his lectures he always reminds us that he's available to talk any time we want, trying to paint himself like some kind of guidance counselor or older brother. Nobody ever takes him up on it. He's half-right, I suppose. I *am* coming to him with a problem, just not the kind he wants, not the kind that has me seeking his advice, something that can make him feel good about himself.

He starts to ask me another question but stops and leans back in his chair to show me that he's relaxed, that there's no pressure here. "Whenever you're ready, Nate," he says. He smiles again, turns his pencil between his fingers.

His composure makes me want to lie to him again. Hell with him, I think. Someone that pleased with himself deserves to be lied to, and for a few moments the gears start to turn, ready to churn out some run-of-the-mill problem, a question of the after-school-special variety. Girls would be the easiest subject; I could tell him I'm confused about the way Lorrie acts sometimes, keep it vague so he can deliver his answers in clichés, give me a fatherly pat on the back, and send me off in time for first period. I know that's my own fear talking, though — a bit of survival instinct trying to change my mind again. And I remember that the last time I was in this office, Coach Harper wasn't the only person who was smug and self-satisfied.

I focus on Marvin and Jackson, the lies I've made them tell, the lies I've told myself. Enough of that.

"I stole the stuff from the fraternity, Coach," I say. *Boom*, it's out like that, no way to take it back now.

Coach Harper lurches forward, the chair legs thudding on the floor, his elbows landing hard on the desk, the pencil springing from his fingers and spinning on the desk.

177

"You what?" he says. "You did what?"

"I stole from the fraternity, from Sigma Chi," I say. The repetition makes it a little more real, and I tag on a perfunctory, "I'm sorry."

He puts his hand to his face with his thumb at one temple and his middle finger at the other, squeezing them slowly together in an arc that swings below his eyes and then brings them up in an aggressive squeeze at the bridge of his nose. When he takes his hand away his face is revealed, his cheeks splotched with small blots of red as his blood rises. His jaw is working hard, like he's chewing my very words. Twitches in his shoulders and hands give him the appearance of a man whose body is beyond his own control, and when he raises his hand it hesitates in the air, as if deciding what direction to take, then slams down flat on his desk, the notepad and pencil performing small jumps, the force of it jolting Coach Harper back in his own chair.

"You son of a *bitch*," he yells, all caution about his language discarded. "You sat right here in my own goddamn office and lied to my face. Who the hell do you think you are?"

His question is not one he wants me to answer, though, because he keeps right on going, barreling forward with a lecture that hits all the things Coach Harper considers important — honesty, respect, responsibility, and teamwork. Not that any of his anger toward me is unjustified, not that anything he says is untrue, but in some ways I expected something else. Coming in I wasn't sure what I thought would happen, but now, as Coach's words start to blend together into a long, singular, and indecipherable scream, I realize I had hoped that admitting my guilt would be some defining moment for me, that it would remove a weight that had hung like a stone around my neck, that I would feel cleansed as if after a long and burdensome journey, that the old saying teachers and parents hand out would be right — that the truth would set me free. I feel none of that, though, and I realize for the first time, even though it should have been clear for months, that there are simply no easy escapes from the traps our own pasts set for us.

"Who else?" Coach yells. "Do you hear me, Nate? I asked you who else was involved." The color in his face is full now, his right hand balled into his left in front of him, as if that's the only way he can control them.

"It was just me," I say. I knew this part would come, and I knew what I'd have to do.

"Jesus, Nate. Don't make it worse. You've lied to me once. Don't do it again. Now, tell me who else was involved."

"Nobody."

His right hand comes up, the index finger snapping at me like a whip. "You're telling me you did that all alone? If you think I believe that, you're an even bigger idiot than I thought you were." The finger jabs toward me, almost to my chest. "Tell me."

"I don't know about anybody else," I say. "I only know what I did. And I'm telling you."

This sends him into another fit. He rips the diagrams from

his notepad and throws them across the room. He slams his fist on the desk. He stands and kicks his own chair so it topples in a clatter. Eventually he runs out of steam and runs his hands through his hair, bends quietly to pick up his chair again, and sits down. When he looks at me all his anger is gone, and he resigns himself to a final soft question: "Was it everyone? Was it the whole team?"

Whatever spite I'd had for him disappears. I understand now that when it came to his players, he had always wanted to believe the best but had suspected the worst the whole time. It wasn't just our team but his, too, and whatever hopes we'd had for the season — all those dreams we'd openly discussed during summer games, all the enthusiasm we brought to practice — were things Coach Harper shared with us. For him, it's already been Trey, now me, and the rest of his roster he must see ready to crumble, like a house hit by a wrecking ball.

"I'm sorry, Coach," I say, and this time I really mean it, discovering sympathy for a man I'd always resented. I'd always seen him as a kind of gatekeeper, an ogre standing between me and a starting spot, but now I see that his own plans are built on teenagers who always let him down, people like me. "I stole from the fraternity, and I'm tired of the rumors swirling about other people. I'm tired of people thinking I'm someone I'm not. I know what this probably means for me, but that's all I came here to tell you."

"Fine, Nate," he says. He seems to surrender, shoulders slumping. He picks his pencil back up and taps it against the table. "Obviously, you're done for the season. Least of your worries at this point, though. As far as everything else, I'll try to sort it out." He sighs and looks away. "Go to class, Nate. I'll take it from here."

I almost start to apologize again, but I've said enough. I head for the door, knowing full well how hard the rest of this day will be. The rest of this semester. The rest of everything.

"I didn't expect it to be you, Nate," he says before I leave. I look back, but he's just staring down at his desk. "There were others I had my doubts about, and I figure I'll find out about them. You might stick up for them, but I'm not that stupid — I know there were others. But, Nate, you were a good kid. Why? I just didn't expect *you*."

I wait a second, wondering if he really wants an explanation, but he just flips his hand at me, motioning me to leave, disgusted. It's a good question, though. Why? It's been long enough now that I can't even remember what I was really thinking that day, why I went along so easily. It could just as well have been another person, someone I knew once but don't recognize anymore. *It doesn't matter,* I tell myself. *I did it. It was me.* As I walk into the hallway, still cold and dark in the November morning, my own footsteps on the cement seem ominous, the stony voice of a judge handing down a sentence, but there is one last thing I can hold on to: I know that from here on out, nobody will blame Marvin for the things I've done.

✻　✻　✻

It takes all the way until third period for the word to get out, almost a record for Cheneysburg. Even if Coach Harper only told his shadow, the news was bound to hit the rumor mill fast. I think the town paper would be better served by stationing a reporter at the corner of junior hall — they'd certainly get their news faster than they do now. I notice it first in the looks I get from random kids in the hall, people I don't even know eyeing me and then looking away quickly. But it's the look I don't get — a quick brush-by from Lorrie, her books clenched tight to her chest, her eyes down — that tells me the word is out.

I try to catch her, tailing behind and calling after her, trying to keep my voice down so I don't make myself more of a spectacle than I already am. I catch up and take a few steps beside her, but she still won't look at me. Then she pivots hard on her heel so she faces me, her eyes down so her bangs conceal part of her face. She huffs and shakes her head. "Just leave me alone," she says.

"Lorrie."

"Just *go*," she says. Her voice rises on the last word, and I feel that unmistakable burn of being stared at. Sure enough, I look around and there are a few people gawking at us in the hallway, a small audience for what should be a private argument.

"We need to talk, Lorrie. I've got to explain."

"Jesus, just go, Nate," she says.

Her eyes flicker up at me and I can tell she's on the verge of tears, so I let it go. I shuffle back to my locker. I sense eyes following me the whole way, as sure as they would be if I were flying down the court on a fast break, ready to put us ahead in the season opener.

Branson is in front of my locker, scratching his arm so hard it brings up red streaks on the flesh. I imagine this has been the nightmare of other students for years, Branson waiting at their lockers with a grudge so big he seems to be wearing it. I'm not in the mood to back down, though, and I try to shove him aside to get to the lock. He leans back with my push, then rocks toward me again, his chest bumping up against me, his face so close I can feel his breath on my neck when he speaks.

"You little fucker," he says. "You sold us out."

I try to concentrate on the spin of my lock, pretending Branson isn't even there. I open the door and drop my books in, pick up a notebook for next period. Branson leans on the door, though, putting his weight behind it so it pinches my arm, and I give an involuntary yelp of pain.

"That hurt?" Branson says. "You're about to feel some more. You just couldn't keep your mouth shut."

"Look, Branson, I didn't tell him anything about anyone else," I say. As I look at Branson, see him scowl, see his biceps beneath his tattered sweater, I want to conjure up some anger and ready myself for a fight, like there's a well of adrenaline that I've always been holding back for this moment. But there's nothing. I've resigned myself to all that's coming my way. "I just admitted to Coach about me. If you have to fight me for that, fine. Whatever you have to do."

183

I see Branson's eyes dart back and forth. "You really didn't say anything about anyone else?" he asks.

"Not a word."

"Okay then," he says. "You're still an idiot. And if I swing for this I swear I will pound your ass into the ground." With that Branson splits, walking fast, like he's hot on a scent.

The rest of the day is a race between Branson and the various school authorities. Between periods I hear players being paged to Principal Cash's office, two or three at a time, and I see Coach Harper working the halls, making sure the players report promptly. Branson also makes the rounds, trying to get to players before Harper and Cash, huddling with them in attempts to hush them up. After lunch, a police cruiser pulls into the parking lot and two cops head for the school offices, their faces all business. I get called out of study hall, the first person the police want to talk to, but I only tell them what I told Coach. Their cruiser stays parked outside the rest of the day, though, and between classes I see people pointing at it, talking low.

For my part, I try to stay as inconspicuous as possible the rest of the day, but each time I hear the loudspeaker crackle — *Trey Vinson, Luke Edwards, Joseph Saveen, please report to Principal Cash's office* — I feel an extra stab of guilt, each name representing someone else I've sold out. The thing is, I knew this would happen. I knew I wouldn't be allowed to take the rap all on my own, but until it all started unraveling, slowly playing out in the Cheneysburg High hallway, I was able to convince myself otherwise. No other players approach me, but I see

184

Branson trying to corral Jackson and I can't help but take a look at how it goes: not well for Branson. Jackson throws away Branson's hand and walks off, and though I can't make out all they say from down the hall, I do hear Branson scream a few profanities as Jackson walks away.

They've got us in the locker room again. Only it's not just Coach Harper and his staff now. The coaches sit off to the side this time, flanked by Principal Cash and a local probation officer. In front of us are the police, stone-faced on simple folding chairs. Even Tuman, the equipment manager, is present this time, his face almost as pale as the gym towel he has flung over his shoulder. Everyone just seems to be waiting for something to happen. Most of the time I keep my head down, but when I look at the police officers I don't even see their faces, just their bulk and shined shoes, their hands on their knees, their guns bulging like knots on a tree, and it's those guns — the heft of them, the shining hammers — that keep my eyes down, scaring me even more than the punishment I know the men carrying the guns have come to deliver.

Behind the police stand three guys I've never seen before, but there's no mystery about who they are. Hair swooped down in a uniform part, expensive sweaters hanging loose beneath leather jackets, a practiced expression — part nonchalance, part disdain — on their faces, and khaki pants leading down to shoes that probably cost more than Coach Harper's best suit: Sigma Chi. I glance over to Branson, who stares insistently at the frat boys, like he's trying to intimidate them. One of them gives him a short nod, his chin jerking to let Branson know that he recognizes his existence, but barely. Branson's stare swings to me then, and I look away.

Coach Harper stands on the side of the room, and his voice is low with shame. "You boys have lied to me. At least most of you. I can't tell you how disappointing that is. Of course, there will be punishment. I'll let the officers give you more on that, but as far as the team, it's pretty simple. Those of you who stole from the fraternity — off the team. Gone for the entire season. Those of you who helped cover it up, normally I'd suspend you, too, but we do need to field a team in a week. So you'll pay for it in wind sprints. And believe me, you will run until you can't feel your legs."

There are murmurs in the locker room, the sounds of players cursing under their breath. Only Branson has the audacity to protest: "But we didn't *do* anything," he says. But even his voice betrays the truth as an adolescent whine sneaks in to replace his normal bullying bass.

Harper runs his tongue across his teeth and squints, amazed at Branson's gall, but when he opens his mouth to respond, the police chief holds up his hand. "I'll field this one," the chief says. Harper nods toward him, then sits down obediently, folding his hands in front of him and hanging his head down, a man who just threw almost every player he has off the team.

The police chief stands with his chest puffed out, like his

186

muscles might burst right through his uniform, and speaks directly at Branson with words popping off like rounds from a rifle. "You are a fool, son. You are a fool if you think you can say that and have any person on God's green earth believe you. You are a fool if you think we came in here on a hunch. What do you think we were doing all day, son?" Branson sits in silence, color draining from his face. "No quick answer for that one," the chief continues. "We have the whole story. And *you* — you with the back way into the fraternity, you with the goods still stacked in the back of that van — *you* are the only one still denying anything. So just be quiet, son."

We look around at one another, some people rolling their eyes in disbelief: Branson never even sold the stuff. We were never going to get our money. But there's no time to get mad, because the chief continues with his lecture, saying he's worked everything out with Coach Harper, Principal Cash, and the representatives from Sigma Chi. He makes it out like a deal he's offering us, but really there's nothing negotiable about it. The charges will be dropped in exchange for community service, which will take the form of cleaning the blocks surrounding the fraternity — picking up litter, painting and repairing some of the nearby buildings, and, worst of all, doing lawn and house maintenance for the fraternity itself. We'll also, as a special measure courtesy of Principal Cash, speak to younger students in the high school and in the middle school system, admitting what we've done and serving as examples of youth gone wrong.

187

So that's what it comes to — they want to make public examples of us. I can picture people driving by while we pick beer cans up off the Sigma Chi lawn, the husband turning to the wife and muttering over the sound of his bad transmission that *those are the boys who got themselves kicked off the team,* or middle schoolers in the back row whispering jokes about us while we talk to them, making our humiliation complete. There is probation, too, which sounds bad at first but amounts to being on a kind of watch list for the police. "One wrong step," the chief warns, like all that stands between us and the state pen is to be on the strip one minute past curfew or to park with our tires nosing across the yellow. No matter how he tries to scare us with tougher penalties on the horizon, it's the public spectacle that gets to me.

"That's the way it shakes out," the chief finishes. "I assume you're okay with that. Unless some of you —" he looks at Branson "— want to fight it, at which point we can haul your ass down to jail."

Nobody says anything this time, not even Branson, who is back to glaring at the fraternity boys. Among some of us there is surely an impulse to fight to the end, go down in that final blaze of glory, cuffed and stuffed on school property, all of Cheneysburg High ogling us, the girls gasping in disbelief, Mr. Davies shaking his head solemnly, Mrs. Marsh's hand to her mouth, her missing finger letting an *oh dear* escape from her lips. But we know our lot now.

We don't get out of the locker room, though, without one

final indignity. The chief turns it over to the boys from Sigma Chi. They look at one another, shrugging, as if it's barely worth their time and effort to be there. Then the one in the center steps forward. His hands are thrust deep in his pockets, and to look at us he has to shake the hair from his eyes with a big twitch.

"I mean, I don't see what you guys were thinking." His voice is deep and lazy, like it's an enormous undertaking to even speak. "We don't ask for much while we're here. We try to stay out of everyone's way and just go about our business. We don't disrespect this town, so I don't see why you'd disrespect us by breaking into our house — our *home* — and robbing us. But we've agreed to this since I suppose there's no sense in getting you guys in more trouble, and besides, you know, the stuff you stole is still around." He stops and gives a half chuckle, impressed by the irony he sees in the situation. "And this way maybe you'll learn something. You know, I guess it's better this way."

He trails off and steps back between his cohorts, his hair falling back in front of his eyes. One of them says something under his breath, and the other two break into wry smiles, shaking their heads. It's enough to make me want to rob them all over again.

Coach Harper dismisses us, and we shuffle out silently. Jackson and the freshmen stay behind for practice, since they now constitute the entire varsity team. Though Harper said we were no longer welcome in the locker room until next year — which means never for the seniors — I pop back in for just a second to find Jackson by his locker.

"I'm sorry," I say. "I know you don't want to hear apologies, but I know I let you down. First in the summer, and now with this."

Jackson, digging through his gym bag for some gear, just shrugs his shoulders. He puts down the bag and looks me in the eyes. "Nate, you'll be okay. You had to deal with what you did, and I can respect that. You didn't rat anyone else out."

"But —"

"Yeah, but you sure as hell opened the floodgates on this thing. It's okay, though. I'll be here when you get back next year. I'll whip these boys into shape by midseason and we'll be fine. You know where I live. So I'll see you around."

I put my fist out to his, but he extends his open hand instead, and when I open my fist he takes my hand solidly in his, gives it a couple shakes.

"Now get out of my locker room, scrub," he says, laughing.

"Shit," I say. "You're just watching the place while I'm out." We slap five, and I turn to make my way out of the locker room, the door sealing the team off behind me. I think of all those jumpers I hoisted over the summer, my quick release that guys like Luke couldn't defend anymore, the additions I've made to my game over the last couple weeks. It seems those are gone, too, as sure as if they were stuffed on the shelves of the equipment room, tucked away behind the deflated volleyballs and broken weight belts.

*   *   *

By the time we get out of the locker room the rest of the school is out and it's only our cars dotting the parking lot. I was hoping to catch Lorrie before she went to practice, but I'll have to talk to her later.

At the south end of the lot, the police are supervising as the fraternity boys retrieve some of their belongings from the back of Branson's van, the rest of which, I assume, are hidden in his house. With each item they unload, they report it to the cops, who seem to be checking a list, and then they pack it carefully into one of their shining SUVs, out of place in a high school parking lot that is usually populated by hand-me-downs and junkers, rarely a vehicle without a cracked window, a botched paint job, or a dent in one of the doors. Of course, there's mine, my dad's ride, which still looks almost new. But after the last few months, I shudder to think of more similarities between me and the fraternity members.

Watching them unload the loot, Branson is leaning against a nearby car and smoking, blowing streams of it into the cold air with disgust. No matter how much I've suffered because of Branson's antics, I can't help but feel a nagging pity. This can't be easy for him. Maybe that's what he reads on my face. Or maybe my mistake was not waiting for him to leave the parking lot before I came out. Either way, he sees me and comes toward me fast, discarding the cigarette and crushing it under his heel on the way. As he crosses the parking lot, I notice other heads turning — the rest of the dismissed players at their respective cars — and a few of them fall in behind Branson at a small distance. For a second I think that this is my retribution in full, that the whole team has turned violently against me.

Branson arrives first. I start to tell him to calm down, that I had no intention of blowing everyone's cover, but this time he's not in the mood to talk. He pops me with his open hand on my shoulder, sending me back into my car. I hold my hand up, almost hoping he'll wait, but he crashes right in on me, one fist following another. I feel blows in my stomach, on the back of my head, my ear, and one on my neck that sends me to the cold pavement, bits of gravel digging into my cheek. I scramble away, not wanting to give Branson a chance to pin me down and do real damage. I feel him grabbing at my coat, trying to pull me back to him, but I tear away and backpedal to put some distance between us. There's no room to run, though, because the other players have crowded around us, some of them shouting at us, and I assume they're urging us on, though I can't make anything out clearly.

"Come here, you little fucker," Branson sneers, looking over to the police to make sure their attention is elsewhere, and are far enough away. "I been wanting this for a while now. Think you can sell us all out and not get a beating?"

Branson comes toward me in small steps, walking in a slight crouch like some animal ready to pounce, his fists rocking back and forth in front of him. He has the look of a practiced fighter, but I can see his chin exposed. I get myself ready, hoping I can pull off one lucky shot, land a blow squarely on that chin and send him reeling, vanquishing the bully like in my childhood daydreams. I remember some of Marvin's friends picking on me as a kid until I was ready to fight, but Marvin always stepped in, made them back off. In my whole life, I've never had to throw a single punch.

I circle away from Branson, but I know I can't delay it forever. Over the shoulders of the other players I can see one of the policemen ambling across the parking lot, leaving the others to oversee the unloading of the van while he checks on our melee. Only he seems to be in no hurry. He shuffles with his hands in the pockets of his jacket, taking his time, as if maybe he's decided to let us fight it out. He probably thinks we all deserve a few punches after what we've done, probably thinks a little primitive law would do us good. And, hell, maybe he's right. Maybe I do deserve what Branson's about to give me. Branson keeps moving in, his eyes squinting, and I curl my hand into a fist, trying to get ready.

It only takes one punch. But it's Branson who goes down and I'm not the one who throws it. When he hits the ground everyone shuts up, only a few sounds lingering as we watch Branson's hands cover his eye where he's been hit, his knees curled up into his stomach. Only Saveen speaks — and since he's the one who dropped Branson, I suppose he has the right.

"That's it, Branson," he says. "You hear me?" He prods at Branson with his foot, only needing a little of his considerable strength to get Branson's attention.

"Fuck you," Branson yells, but it almost comes out as a sob, guttural and broken. "Why the fuck you hit *me*? Fuck you!"

Saveen kicks Branson in the ribs, just hard enough to shut him up, make his hands shoot from his face down to his chest, and when Branson's face is revealed, we can already see red where he's been hit. There are also splotches of red on his cheeks, his embarrassment rising. I feel that earlier pity again, stronger this time.

"Shut up!" Saveen says. "Jesus, just shut up. It's over, okay? There's no sense in you beating up Nate when you're the one who started this whole damn thing. It's over."

"No," Branson says, quieter now. "No. You can't do this."

"It's over," Saveen says again. He presses his foot onto Branson's chest, and there's no protest this time.

The cop finally makes it to our gathering, poking his head into the middle of it. He walks up to Saveen and puts a hand on his shoulder. Saveen ducks his shoulder out from the policeman's touch, a brisk, defiant motion, but he backs off of Branson and recedes into the rest of us. The policeman bends over Branson and asks him if he's okay, and Branson just nods, getting to his feet and brushing dirt from his jeans.

"That's it, boys," the cop says. "Don't make things worse. Go home. I'm sure your parents want to talk to you, too."

We shuffle off, each of us probably already plotting out the things we'll try to tell our parents: the half denials, the justifications, the tearful apologies. Whatever works to get by.

I pat Saveen on the back in an unspoken thank-you, but

when I look at him he just shakes his head. Even though he saved me from Branson, it will take some time before he wants to talk to me. Branson won't look at anyone, but he keeps rubbing at his eyes and nose, and I know he's fighting back tears. Not from the blows he took — I know Branson's tougher than that — but because Saveen is right; it *is* over: the whole charade, the struggle, the stranglehold Branson had on the team, and I realize now what I've done to him. For some things there are no apologies.

Chapter 16

My parents break my heart, in their own way. When I get home they're sitting side by side on the couch, waiting for me. There's something sadly orderly about it, like they think this is the proper way to go about it, team up like the parenting combination they haven't been in years, plaster looks of deep concern on their faces. There's no hint of their afternoon drinks, no noise coming from the television. They're all business.

"Talk to me, Son," my father says. All ears, all compassion.

I sink down on the chair across from them. I see the remote on the table beside me and ache to turn on the television, anything but this. As far as I'm concerned, I'd rather just get handed the punishment and be left alone. "What am I supposed to say?" I ask.

"We need to talk about this, Nathan," he says. "We need to know how all this happened." His voice stays calm, but it can't fool me: I know they're mad as hell.

My mother leans closer, looking at me. "What happened to you? What happened to your face?"

"Some guys don't like it when you get them busted," I say.

"Hey," my father says. "You're in no position to be a smart-ass right now. We're trying to be understanding, so just act like an adult for once."

I sigh, but straighten up in my seat, look them in the eye. He has a point, I suppose. "Branson hit me, but, really, I can understand why."

"Was he the same boy that made you all do it?" my mother says.

She's opened the door. Not that there will be any easy escape, but the way she said it makes it seem so simple — he *made* us do it. No Branson, no robbery. No robbery, no guilt. No problem. I see the look my dad gives her, though, and I know he's not about to fall for an explanation that simple.

"It was his idea," I say. "But, I mean, we still did it. Branson's strong, but he doesn't have the heft to make nine guys do what he wants. Besides, Jackson didn't get involved. I mean, if he was smart enough to leave, then I guess I could have been, too."

"Jackson?" my father says. "Jackson didn't have anything to do with it? He's not kicked off the team?"

"No," I say. There's a squint to my father's face I don't trust, like it's implying more than he wants to. "What's that supposed to mean, anyway? I mean, why are you surprised Jackson didn't do anything wrong?"

He leans forward. "Watch your tone, boy. Now I might not throw you around like those fathers down on the avenues, but I'll be goddamned if I'll take any shit from you today. I don't have to explain things to you."

I sink back in my chair, look away from him. I see the

197

bookshelf, the pictures on the mantel, the newest painting my mother hauled back from Indianapolis, the end table, the candles. Everything in its place, polished, just so. I can barely take it.

"At least you're not trying to shove the guilt on someone else," he says. "I'll give you that. But that doesn't change the fact you're a damn criminal, and everybody knows it. How's that going to look? God. My one son a thief and my other . . ." He trails off, his eyes wide like he's surprised himself with where that sentence was going, almost saying out loud what he must have been thinking all this time.

My mother looks down, swallowing hard. She picks at a loose thread on the couch cushion. "Honey," she says. She stands and walks to my dad, starts running her hand across his back, her mouth open like she's trying to think of the next thing to say. He stays tense for a few seconds, and then his shoulders go slack, kind of surrendering to her tenderness. He puts his hand on hers and lets it linger there for a moment, turning to look at her. Between them, some secret transmission seems to take place, like they can read each other's thoughts and reach some silent understanding. She nods at him and slips out of the room, barely making a sound with her steps.

He watches her walk away, following her with his eyes until she turns the corner, and then he swings his head back to me slowly and without menace, as if he has noticed me sitting here for the first time.

"Go, Nate," he says.

"That's it?"

He sighs, a deep and exhausting noise, as if he is exhaling all his years in Cheneysburg, trying to blow them away from him like clinging sand. He runs his hand through his hair, leaving it tangled on his head in a gray swirl. "Like you said, Nate, what are we supposed to say? Coach Harper called me today, explained the whole thing, how everything came out. You know it's wrong. You know we're disappointed, that you've hurt us. You won't be leaving this house any time soon except for school, I can promise you that. But Jesus, Nate, I'm just tired. Screaming and yelling isn't going to do anything new for us, won't do any better than it's done for any other father and son."

"Okay," I say. In a way, I could handle more shouting better than this. My defenses have been up all day, and I know my dad can't throw anything at me that's worse than Branson's fists. But his quiet, his resignation, his *pain* over what I've done is harder to take — like with Coach Harper, I only considered my father in terms of the punishment he could hand me, never considering that I could, in fact, hurt him.

I feel old as I stand, and I can feel the bruises from Branson's punches. I imagine I rise so slowly I look like an arthritic agonizing over every movement.

"You okay?" my father says.

"Fine," I say. "I'm lucky it's not worse. Branson could have crushed me if Saveen hadn't stepped in." Now that he doesn't want me to talk, I feel an urge to explain everything, to give him a detailed account of all that's happened. Mostly, I suppose, I want to tell him about Marvin, about how my brother's the

199

one who helped me understand what I'd done, how he's put his life together well enough to move to Chicago and escape Cheneysburg, from his history here, from us. My father doesn't react, though, just watches me as I leave the room, hobbling a little when I feel a sting in my knee from where it hit the pavement, the sensation not unlike a floor burn from diving after a loose ball, a feeling that's usually satisfying, accompanied by a scab that serves as a badge for hustle. But there are no badges now.

"Why'd you *do* it?" my father asks. I'm almost out of the room when he says it, spitting the words out with a pent-up disgust, the way our coaches might get one last dig at us when we're about to leave the locker room after a disappointing loss. "What were you *thinking?*"

"I don't know, Dad," I say. I turn back to him, see his head at a tilt as he inspects me, his collar unbuttoned and loose. "I don't know. It's like I was scared not to."

He shakes his head at that answer, almost laughs. He grunts and walks to the kitchen with his head down.

It takes a few calls before Lorrie will talk. I imagine her parents watching her answer the phone three times in a five-minute period. I'm sure they know what's going on, that it's me calling, and each time I dial I half-expect one of them to answer the phone angrily, give me the dreaded parental *don't ever call here again*. But they don't. It's always Lorrie. Maybe her parents are still testing each other, each daring the other to make the first move so it can be criticized later, red-flagged, like a debt in their crumbling marriage.

"Will you *stop*?" Lorrie says. "You can't keep calling here. My parents are mad enough already."

"At you?" I say.

"Well, mainly at *you*, Nate. I mean, I'm not the one who stole nine thousand dollars' worth of goods from Sigma Chi." The number staggers me, the first time I've heard it tallied as a total. I had no idea we'd taken that much stuff, but then I think back to those repeated trips to Branson's van, the way a few guys started standing by the back door to load stuff in neatly, setting up a human conveyor belt.

"But they're not exactly thrilled with me, either," she continues. "They think I knew about it." I start to remind her that she *did* know about it, after the fact, but all I get out is a knowing *well* before she cuts me off. "Don't say it. Don't you dare say it, Nate."

"Are they listening?" I ask.

"No. They're in their bedroom. And I can always tell if someone else is on the line."

"How are they doing?" I ask.

On the other end she just groans, pure frustration with me. I can almost see her eyes rolling, the small ripples of muscle in her arms flexing as she puts her hand to her head in disbelief. I feel a pang of loss, knowing that she might not want to see me anymore, that even if she does I won't be able to go out with her.

"Just hang up," Lorrie says. "Don't think you can call here after what you did and just make small talk about my parents. Don't be an asshole, Nate."

"That's not *small talk*," I say. I can hear my voice getting defensive, so I slow down, try to make it calm. I don't have much room for error now. "I really meant that. I know it's something that's been hard for you."

She sighs. "Fine, Nate. Whatever. They're actually doing better. I mean, there are still some weird spells where they seem to be insinuating something every time they speak, but every once in a while I catch them laughing and touching each other, like they're flirting again. They'll probably be okay."

"See," I say. "Things can work out."

She groans again, almost growls, insulted by my very suggestion. "Not everything, Nate. What the hell were you thinking? I told you this is how it would be, that I wasn't dating you so everyone could think I was with some criminal. I can't see you anymore."

"Give me a chance," I say.

"I did."

We don't say anything then, and I have to fight back images from the summer: Lorrie's face looking down at me in the pool, her neck tilted gently as she looked up at the eclipse, the feel of her hand tracing along my stomach as we reclined against my car out by Bethel Bridge, her deft maneuvers as she threw on the T-shirt her mother had forbidden and slithered out of her blouse, her skin always smoothed by light, from the pool, the moon, the passing streetlights.

"Is this your decision or your parents'?" I ask.

"Mine," she says.

"I don't believe you."

"You don't have to."

"Then you were just going out with me for who people thought I was? Not because you actually liked me?"

I hear her tongue pop against the roof of her mouth, and she slams something — maybe her fist thumping down on her mattress. I can almost see her eyes flash with anger. "That's not fair!" she says.

She hangs up, not even giving me a chance to respond. She doesn't even slam the phone, though, just sets it back down so there's a feeble click, which seems more like a hiccup in the conversation than a final note.

I start to dial again, my fingers punching the first six digits quickly, having built up a pretty good rhythm after the first few times I had to dial. I've called so many times over the years that my hand knows the feel of it, like the motion of dialing is built into my head now, as if it were my own personal sign language for *Lorrie* rather than a pattern that corresponds to the digits in her phone number. Before the seventh number I wait, though, my finger coming to a gentle rest on the last digit. Maybe I should just let her be. I suppose I've put her through enough, and I don't see how I can change her mind tonight. But for some reason I still feel an urgency about calling her, like if I don't push down that last number now I'll never get a chance to talk to her again. My parents certainly won't let me out of the house for a date any time soon, and I can't see Lorrie's parents letting her come over here.

There's a soft knock at the door, the hesitant sound of my mother. That last digit in Lorrie's number never gets pressed, and I toss the phone on the bed and tell my mother to come in, though all she does is swing the door halfway open and stand in the entrance, the dark hallway stretching out behind her.

"You can come on *in*," I say. She looks down, nervously wipes her palms on the front of her slacks. Raising her head again, she still doesn't look directly at me, picking a spot over near my window to look at. It's like she thinks everything is an intrusion: her knock on the door, her body in my room, even her eyes. I cringe inside, knowing this is because of the tone I had when I spoke, because of the tone I always take with her — a husband's silence and a son's sneer making her feel like a trespasser in her own home. "I'm sorry," I say. "I didn't mean it that way."

"That's okay, Nate," she says. She gives a nervous smile and crosses her arms at her chest. "I just wanted to let you know dinner's ready soon." She looks down again and frowns, like she's fretting over a stain on my carpet. "I remember when you were a boy and you and Marvin would . . ."

She trails off, leaving his name hanging there, the first time I can remember her uttering it in years. I wait for her to continue, then ask her to finish what she was saying, knowing that she had something specific in mind, some story from my youth, when everything fit together in this house — the day Marvin taught me to ride my bike, the year my father bought a set of season tickets for the Pacers, the times they let us stay up late during their parties, Marvin and I fighting to stay awake on the couch while the adults reveled. I can remember how young my mother looked then, some color still in her face, how my father would come over to her with his hair a little tousled, put an arm around her waist, and give her a sloppy kiss on the cheek, how their friends would laugh and my mother would blush. I want that. I want her to remember it, too, to talk about it even for a few minutes so we can go back there, music on the stereo and the sound of ice tumbling into glasses, the reaction to someone spilling a drink in the kitchen, a crowd freezing around it momentarily, as if in a picture, and then rushing to clean the mess while my father reignites the levity by saying *cut that man off* even while he pours him another cocktail. I want to talk about the game Marvin and I would play of edging close to the action while trying not to attract attention, so we could continue staying up, like if we shattered the barrier of bedtimes by enough distance we could actually stop the effects of time.

She won't do it, though. She just shakes her head gently and rubs her temples as if she's trying to rid herself of a nagging headache. "We're not as angry as you think," she says. "I'm sorry if it seems that way."

I realize that if we're ever going to talk about Marvin in this house again — really talk and not let the subject quietly haunt us — that I'm the one that has to do it.

"I've talked to him," I say. Her eyes narrow, and I realize she doesn't know what I mean, doesn't know who *him* is. "I went to Marvin's place. A couple times. He saw us rob the fraternity, and he's a big part of the reason I finally came clean."

She starts to react, but her lips tremble slightly, unable to form words. She doesn't know what to do with her hands, folding them in front of her, then putting them at her sides before finally taking a few steps toward me and sitting on the edge of my bed so she can fold them innocently in her lap. Finally she asks quietly, "How is he?"

"He's good," I say. "At least he's a million times better than he used to be. He's not the guy people make him out to be."

She brings her fingers to her lips, but behind them I can see the beginning of a smile at hearing news about her son. It's tentative, though, as if she doesn't trust even the slightest happiness. She looks toward the door, perhaps afraid my father will come in to discover us having this forbidden conversation. Earlier, I had wanted to have the same conversation with him, but I froze up. It was like I had to get warmed up to the idea, the way some players try to envision their performance on the court before the game actually starts. But, more than that, I know how much my mom needed to hear about Marvin; through all the silence, the blaming of herself and others, the medication for her nerves, what she really wanted was to know that Marvin was okay.

206

"Would he see us?" she asks. She blinks fast, trying to keep her emotions in check.

I tell her I don't know, but that whatever anger Marvin used to have seems pretty well spent. But then I have to add that he is planning on moving again, this time away from Cheneysburg, and when I give her this news she looks down and begins nervously smoothing my bedspread. I want to tell her there is time to see him, to convince him to stay, but I have learned enough to make no more promises that I'm not sure I can keep.

"Can I tell your father?" she asks. At first it sounds like I'm the parent and she's asking permission, but she explains. "I mean, I should tell him this first. It's going to be hard, but I know he'll want to hear. Nate, I know Marvin leaving was hard on you — and maybe you blame your father for it. But you can't know how painful it was for him. Nobody can possibly understand that. Let me be the one to tell him, okay?"

I promise her that, knowing I can live up to that much. Then we're quiet, too nervous to look at each other. Normal mothers and sons wouldn't hesitate to hug each other, say that they love each other, but even if we've broken through the barrier of silence surrounding Marvin, we're a long way from being a happy family. She smoothes the bedspread one more time, mutters that she should check on dinner, and slips out the door.

It's an exit — muted, uncomfortable — not unlike any other she had made from my room in the last few years, but I can feel the change in the room, everything in it seeming like its true self for the first time.

Chapter 17

This is the night. Season opener, and the gym is juiced, just like I imagined a million times over: Lorrie with her friends near the scorer's table, her knees bouncing in anticipation; the seats under the north basket packed with the tough men from the mills, some of their cheeks red with whiskey, the farmers crowding around them, cheering each Cheneysburg starter as he's introduced; the railings above lined with suits, the businessmen fresh off putting the finishing touches on a working week, throwing popcorn into their mouths while they look down on the scene like they're still a little too refined to be in the thick of the crowd, the rest of the town in a sprawl below them; the cheerleaders pumping their arms toward the crowd from the edge of the court, the pleats in their skirts teasing away from their thighs with each little excited hop; the student body rising in a sea of blue behind our bench; the opposing fans in a conspicuous sliver of red that seems to jag into the corner of the arena like a blade; the stoners under the south hoop, the only section of the crowd not on their feet yet, waiting at least until the game starts to go through the effort of showing emotion.

Only it's not like I planned at all. I was supposed to be out there, running toward midcourt and bumping fists with Saveen, Luke, Trey, and Jackson while the crowd cheered us to get the tip. I was supposed to be flaring off screens, getting the ball right in rhythm from Jackson and knocking down jumper after jumper. I was supposed to be one of the five digging in on defense, helping down into the post and then recovering back to the perimeter, getting stop after stop. But that's only how I expected it to be, not how it really is. Instead, I'm standing in the corner of the arena, in the hollow spot between the bleachers and the seats off the sideline, and I'm only out of the house because my father gave me a pass for a night, telling me how when he was a kid he got into trouble for lifting records from a local music store, slapping me on the knee, and saying, "You ought to be at that gym tonight, one way or the other." So I am, tucked back where I can see everyone but where they won't notice me.

As the centers get ready to jump, though, I feel a presence behind me, and I turn to see Saveen, his chest almost up against me. I say hello to him, but he just nods toward the court, where the action's starting. We're starting four freshmen and Jackson, a huge mismatch against a perennial power like North Workston, and sure enough they get the tip. North Workston dumps it straight down into the post, and their big man wheels and drops in a quick jumper over our freshman center. The crowd, which was completely amped, quiets and sits, while North Workston's section stands in unison, cheering.

They'd love nothing more than to blow us out to start the season, the same way last season ended.

"Shit, I would have swatted that," Saveen says. It's true, too. No way does a kid make an easy bucket like that against Saveen. "Come on, Jackson," he yells, cupping his hands to his mouth. He's loud enough that a few people look down from the stands and see us. I think I see Lorrie glare my way, but she turns her head back to the game so quick I can't be sure if she noticed me. From the bleachers beside us I hear a few grumbles, like people are pointing out me and Saveen, the delinquents who ruined the team. The others are here, too, even Trey making it out of the house for the big game. I saw the players as I walked in, most of them with their parents, looking forlorn. In a way, it's a punishment to watch the game and know that we could make a difference if we were out there — but the one constant in Cheneysburg, no matter who's playing or who's been kicked off or how lopsided the matchup might be, is that you come to the basketball game on Friday night.

On the other end, the team works patiently for a shot, the freshmen looking flustered each time they catch the ball, pressured way out on the perimeter, but Jackson cuts to the middle each time to get the ball and reset the offense. Finally he cuts to the middle and his man overplays, going for a steal and ending up out of position, so Jackson spins back toward the basket and drives into the lane; then when he draws two more defenders he calmly drops a dime to a forward who lays it in to tie the score. The crowd goes nuts and Coach Harper claps from the sideline, nodding in approval like everything's going according to plan.

Without thinking, I turn and slap five with Saveen, as sure as if he'd been the one who made the shot. He doesn't even hesitate in returning my enthusiasm. Back on the court, we surprise North Workston with a full-court press, and they throw it away. We get it to Jackson, who quickly drops in a jumper to give us a lead. Again the crowd goes wild, the people below the baskets stomping on the bleachers in a frantic rhythm, and for a few extraordinary minutes the game continues to go like that: North Workston turns it over or misses a bunny, and we immediately get the ball in Jackson's hands, who either takes it straight to the hoop or starts into the offense, each time running it until we get a wide-open look. Finally North Workston is forced to call a time-out, down 14–4, the crowd at a fever pitch.

I turn to Saveen, who's smiling, and we slap five again. "God, I wish I was out there," I say.

"Me, too, brother," he says.

There's a lull between us then, and I look down at my feet, feeling like the whole crowd is staring at us, even though I'm sure they're more interested in the game.

"You talk to anyone else on the team?" I ask.

"Yeah, I still talk to Trey and Luke. And I apologized to Branson for beating his ass. Don't take this the wrong way, but none of them want to talk to you. They'd be pissed if they saw me here next to you."

I look away, see Lorrie in the crowd. I know she notices me

this time, because she does a quick double take in my direction before turning back to her friends, jumping into whatever conversation they're having. I have the urge to walk over there, sit down next to her just like I should be able to, like she was still my girlfriend and I had every right, but I can't do that to her — cause a scene when she just wants to be able to act normal with her friends at the game.

"I should have listened to Lorrie," I say. "She didn't want me to tell anyone. I could have saved everyone a lot of trouble."

Saveen puts a hand on my shoulder. "Shiiit," he says. "I suppose I could have listened to Lorrie, too."

"What?"

"Well, she wanted me to be a man, to stand up to Branson. If I had done that during the summer, none of this would have happened."

I turn to him again and shake my head. "That's not fair to yourself, Saveen."

Saveen shrugs his shoulders and shoves his hands in his pockets. He looks at the crowd gathered for the game, almost half the town packed into the arena, and he seems to be talking about all of it when he speaks. "Not much of anything is fair," he says.

The buzzer sounds to bring the teams back out for action, and the crowd rises again. In their noise, I hear someone shouting my name, but can't place it. Finally I see Marvin halfway up the bleachers, sitting next to some people I've never seen before.

"What are you doing down there, little man?" he says.

Before I can answer, he ducks under the railing, dangles his feet down, and jumps about five feet right next to me, as nimble as a kid on the park's jungle gym, the kid I can still remember him being. "What," he says, "you finally decide what to do and you don't come by to see me anymore?"

I start to protest, but he stops me and says he was only joking. "I've been busy; otherwise I would have called you, Nate. I'm proud of you."

"I would have called you," I say. "Dad's monitoring my phone time pretty tight, though."

I introduce Marvin to Saveen, but it's clear they both know each other already — Saveen recognizing Marvin from infamy, and Marvin recognizing Saveen from his fame at this very court. Marvin nods at the court. "I think your man Jackson might pull off a miracle tonight."

But as he says it one of the freshmen turns the ball over and North Workston gets an easy fast break: 14–6.

I tell Marvin I thought he'd be in Chicago by now and hope that maybe he's not going after all. I realize that my deepest hope, even though I barely admitted it to myself, was that because of my coming clean about the theft Marvin would stay. I thought maybe by breaking apart the team, tearing down my own reputation, I could keep Marvin here, put other things back together. There's no logic in that, I understand now: Once things are broken, they stay broken. Marvin tells me he'll be on his way soon, at least by the end of the month.

My mother has been slow to act since our discussion; it took her several days to work up the nerve to tell Dad, but I suppose after spending years getting used to Marvin being gone, it would take a few days to get used to the fact that he wasn't completely out of their lives, at least not yet. Still, I was worried that maybe our chance to bring Marvin back into the family had slipped away. Now, I realize the opportunity is still there.

"You should come see Mom and Dad before you leave," I say. I try to make it sound natural, like it's a friendly suggestion for him to stop by before he goes on a weekend trip.

Marvin sighs at the suggestion, though. He runs his tongue across his teeth and shakes his head. "Nate, I don't know if I can do that. I don't know if they want to see me."

"Mom would, I know. I told her I talked to you."

Marvin raises his eyebrows at that news, impressed with my directness. He nods a few times, thinking over his prospects. "Just give it time, Nate," he says. "It's a lot easier to imagine us getting along again than it is for that to actually happen, but keep giving us time."

He looks me in the eye, waiting for my reaction until I nod in agreement.

On court, Cheneysburg is beginning to unravel. North Workston drops in a three, steals the inbounds pass, and buries another three: 14–12. Coach Harper calls time-out, and I see frustration flash across Jackson's face He immediately suppresses it, walks over to the player who threw the ball away, and calmly instructs him on what he should have done instead, trying to hold things together.

214

It goes on like that after the time-out. We make a bucket or two, maybe make a small run, but eventually our flaws show through, and even Jackson's passionate play — he dives on the floor; he defends relentlessly; he makes the right shots and passes; he never comes out for a break — can't prevent the inevitable. North Workston pulls away slow, but it's evident they'll end. The only thing in doubt is the margin of victory.

I can feel it all slipping away, the things I wanted eroding as we move forward into the lives we all have. I can't see the future now, can't even imagine what it will hold. I think of it now like someone exploring a burned-out house, salvaging what he can — a half-preserved picture, the image clouded by smoke. Then Marvin takes me by the elbow and leans close. "You know," he says, "whether I visit or not, you should know that Dad won't ground you forever. There will be a time when you can hop in your car and come visit me for a weekend."

It fixes nothing, but it does give me something to hold on to — a new idea of the future. I think about barreling up I-65, seeing the city loom on the horizon. I try to imagine Lorrie riding shotgun, in charge of the directions and the music selections. I try to think of us as different people, almost as adults. I turn the phrase *a weekend in the city* over in my head, testing its fit.

North Workston keeps pulling away, up fourteen points at halftime. When the second half resumes, I know nothing will change. There is no going back, and whatever magic Cheneysburg captured at the beginning of the game is vanished and irretrievable. They can't wind the clock back and start over, retrace their steps. It doesn't work that way. But I know Jackson will keep playing hard, teaching the freshmen, building on this game for the next and then the next, trying to forge something out of the season. And for now, I'm content watching it — always wishing that I was out there to help, that things had happened differently — analyzing the game next to my brother, who I will visit in his new life, and my friend Saveen, who has the courage to still stand beside me even if I couldn't do the same for him.

To the rest of the crowd, we are practically invisible, and I don't mind being forgotten, the shadows suiting me fine for this night. Only Lorrie keeps looking over in distraction, like she's trying to signal something to me, but I'm too far away to read her eyes. I see her looking at Marvin sometimes, and then she'll stare down at her hands before turning back to the game, clapping and urging the team on, like she's trying hard to focus on it. I'll go to her games this winter, too, staying again on the periphery, since I'm sure that's where she wants me.

Marvin gets drinks for the three of us, tosses us each a bag of popcorn fresh from the concession stand, and we get caught up in discussing the team. Saveen thinks some of the freshmen have a chance to come on strong, and Marvin thinks we'll have to play some zone this year to protect them defensively. I stand back and listen to them, enjoying the simple pleasure of a brother's company and trying not to dwell on all that's happened. Then I see Lorrie stand during a time-out, walk down her row of seats like she's headed for the concession stand, too. When she gets to the corner of the seats, just down the baseline from us, she pauses there, not looking in our direction or at the concession stand, staring down instead at her feet, as if she's waiting for them to decide her direction.

Marvin notices me looking at her and gives me a little nod of encouragement. *Go ahead,* he seems to be saying, the same reassurance he used to give me when I was a kid, getting into a pickup game with the older boys. *Nothing to worry about.* He tells me this without having to say a word, and I think about crossing the gym to Lorrie, walking right in front of the bleachers where everyone can see me, but something is still holding me back. It's as if I'm afraid to walk to Lorrie, afraid to take a step in my own shadow.

I can feel the hot gym lights above me, and they cast a long outline of my body across the floor, making the distance between us seem to stretch out like a canyon. But it is no greater than the distance I've covered to understand Jackson, to reach Marvin, to discover who I really am beneath the person I pretended to be. I walk toward her, unafraid of anyone watching.